The World of the Jaguar

PERRY, Richard. The world of the jaguar. Taplinger, 1970. 168p il
map bibl 78-117933. 6.50. ISBN 0-8008-8590-2

Perry is fast gaining a reputation as an outstanding writer of volumes
dealing with larger mammals. To his previous list of books pertaining
to the tiger, polar bear, panda, walrus and red deer, he has added a
comprehensive study of the jaguar and a thorough review of its natural
history. The jaguar is still to be found in the more remote areas of
Central and South America and Perry writes as if he has spent much
time studying this big cat in its native habitat. Perry quotes extensively from the diaries of early explorers and hunters to delineate the
background against which he accurately portrays the behavior of the
jaguar. Behavioral patterns, feeding habits and relations with man are
detailed with a blessed lack of anthropromorphisms and sentimentality.
The jaguar preys not only on the ground but in trees, feeding on sloths
and monkeys, and in swamps and rivers. Thus, the jaguar is one of the
main predators of the Amazon River Basin. This area is the setting for
accounts of encounters with the anaconda, piranhas, tapir, peccary,
anteaters and capybara. There is no new data of interest to a professional mammologist in this book, but it can serve as a model for
presenting data to interested laymen in   aightforward and ab-

PERRY

sorbing manner. Rather unusual for a book of this type, there is a
complete index, five page bibliography, list of scientific names of animals mentioned in the text and a series of above average photographs.

Other Books by Richard Perry

The World
of the Jaguar

by Richard Perry

TAPLINGER PUBLISHING COMPANY
NEW YORK

First published in the United States in 1970 by
TAPLINGER PUBLISHING CO., INC.
New York, New York 10003

ISBN 0-8008-8590-2

Library of Congress Catalog Card Number 78-117-933

Printed in Great Britain

Contents

List of Illustrations

1

The Jaguar in his Country

Fly north of east from the Tehachepi Mountains (north of Los Angeles) to the Grand Canyon in Arizona, and then south-east to the delta of the Colorado on the Gulf of Mexico. Your flight will have demarcated the northern boundary of the jaguar's known range. Fly on south from the Gulf for 5,000 miles, over the seemingly endless rain-jungles of Central America and Amazonia, the vast savannas, swamps and jungle of the Mato Grosso, and the pampas of Argentina, until you reach the Rio Negro and the jaguar's most southerly marches.

There are still many jaguars in the mangrove swamps along the west coast of Mexico and in the dense tropical *monte* of rain-forest in the foothills; while in the remaining forests of the Gulf coast there are still too many for livestock to range freely. Indeed, according to a contemporary American naturalist, Starker Leopold, herds being driven along dim trails through the virgin forest to the market at Tabasco face the hazard of night attacks by jaguars when they straggle, resulting in heavy losses not only among cattle, but also among horses, mules, burros, goats and sheep.

There must still be great numbers of jaguars in the inconceivably immense forests and swamps of Amazonia's two million square miles; and still more in the Pantanal of the southern Mato Grosso, that other half million square miles of steaming jungle and swamp, of lakes with islets of palms and *tarumas,* of long winding canal-like ditches or *bayous,* of clear black gleaming streams free of algae and miasmic slime, but with beds of floating plants as fiercely fresh a green as the grass on the blue ridges of

9

the savannas to the north, where thick woods border the ranches of the cattle-men. Mato Grosso: that vast primeval sponge (in Julian Duguid's words) absorbing the Rio Paraguay's perennial floods—trackless for the most part to all but the few Indians, whose numbers are still unknown.

There were jaguars on the formerly tree-less pampas of Argentina, lairing in reed-beds and low brush and, if these were not available, in the earths of wild dogs, if the eighteenth-century naturalist, F. de Azara, is to be believed. There are jaguars high in the *montana* and *cordillera* of the eastern Andes. Richard Spruce found them common at a height of 3,000ft around Tarapoto in Peru, where their skins, and also those of pumas, were so abundant that one could be obtained in exchange for a knife or a handkerchief. W. H. Osgood saw the tracks of one at 7,000ft in northern Peru, and that is generally believed to be as high as they range. Nevertheless, C. H. Prodgers, the adventurer, found jaguars in numbers in the country of the Challana outlaws between the Coroico and the Andes some 9,000ft up in the Bolivian *cordillera*, despite the fact that the 24 hour temperature differential ranged from minus 40° F to plus 80° F. These short-haired jaguars, preying on feral cattle in the forest and on the Indians' mules and pack-llamas, were thriving in conditions comparable to those experienced by the long-furred tigers in Manchuria.

When considering the geographical range of a predatory animal one tends to think of this as being influenced by climate and terrain. But a predator lives where prey is plentiful; climate and terrain are of secondary importance in his choice of habitat. Jaguars are typically denizens of rain-jungle, marsh and river bank: but they can subsist in the near-desert country of the central Mexican plateau or the Mojave in California; on the drought-stricken tablelands of sand, rock and thorn jungle in north-eastern Brazil's cattle country; in the arid scrub-jungle of the Quintana Roo's almost waterless limestone, where they lair in the ancient temples of the Maya buried in the jungle; or on the cool and comparatively waterless pampas.

There are, of course, other factors that will take a predator

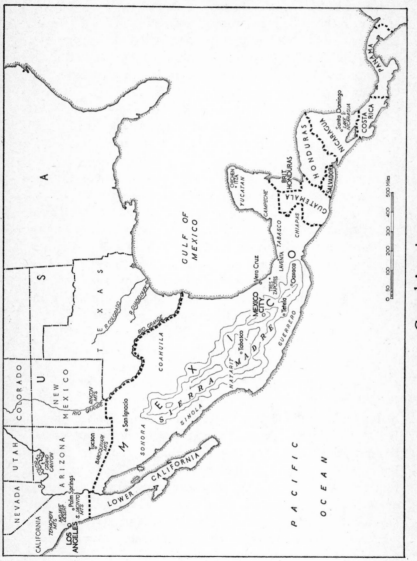

Central America

out of its normal habitat. The hunting grounds available to predators in South America are so vast that territorial pressures are not likely to be experienced by the general run of jaguars, and it was surely human pressures that forced the jaguars out of the jungle on to the Argentine pampa, for Azara stated that as many as 2,000 were being killed annually in the valley of the La Plata in the early years of the Spanish Conquest. Territorial pressures in the east and west lowlands of Mexico may, however, be responsible for those instances of individual jaguars migrating far up the gorges of large rivers into the montane pine forests. An adult male, which was killed in September 1955 near the southern tip of the San Pedro Martyr range in Baja, California, 500 miles from the nearest regularly occupied jaguar country, could only have reached this locality by traversing the full extent of the Sonoran desert and then crossing the Colorado river and bearing south for 100 miles. No doubt most of these wandering jaguars are males, with strongly developed migratory impulses. Nevertheless, there is irrefutable evidence by John Capen Adams, the grizzly-bear hunter, of a pair of jaguars rearing young in the Tehachepi Mountains in 1855 despite, as in central Mexico, the unfavourable Californian terrain of mountain ranges separated by mesquite-covered plains and semi-deserts; but this is the only record of jaguars breeding in the USA beyond the marshes of tropical south-east Texas.

Evidence regarding the migratory tendencies of jaguars is sparse and conflicting. Richard Schomburgk stated that in British Guiana they wandered extensively, especially up into the mountains, except during the mating season. This was also the experience of a contemporary zoologist, B. S. Wright, who found that they might roam hundreds of miles from their home ground, as did the San Pedro male; while Theodore Roosevelt asserted that in the Taquari marshes of Paraguay individual jaguars habitually covered a wide and irregular range, passing a day or two here, a week there, if water was adequate and game plentiful—the deciding factor—as the Indian tiger does. This was also the opinion of George Cherrie, a very sound naturalist and vastly experienced explorer who made no fewer than

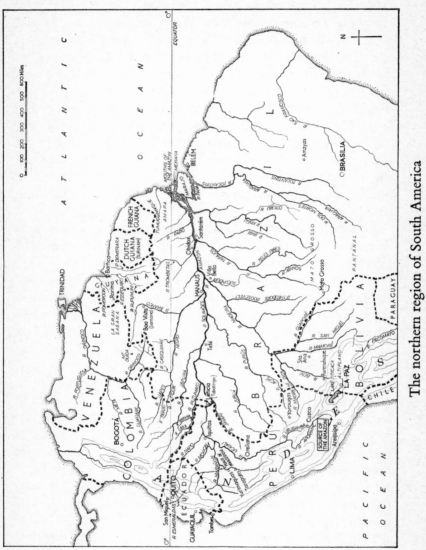

The northern region of South America

thirty-eight expeditions to South America. Leopold, on the other hand, says that the belief that jaguars range far and wide every night when hunting is based erroneously on the fact that they are known to run great distances when hunted by hounds; and according to the guide J. F. Ferreira, who hunted jaguars for forty years in Sinaloa on the north-west coast of Mexico, those in the San Ignacio region confine themselves, when undisturbed, to very small territories of no more than from two to five kilometres, in which they are normally to be found.

That territorial rights are strictly enforced in densely populated areas (though the female's range may overlap those of the males), would seem to be confirmed by the success of hunting methods based on attracting jaguars by imitating their roar.

Jaguars, like other cats, keep the striking talons on their forefeet sharp by stretching up on their hind legs and drawing the talons down the trunks of certain favoured trees, thus ridding them of ragged portions or even of complete sheaths of outer horn. The Gauchos showed Charles Darwin three of these claw-sharpening trees on the banks of the Uruguay. Grooved scratches, almost a yard long, and of different ages, extended obliquely from the central part of each tree on which the bark had been worn smooth by the 'embraces' of jaguars. Thirteen years later, however, Darwin conjectured that this practice might be a ritualised replacement for roaring as a means of indicating territorial boundaries; and a contemporary zoologist has improved upon this fantasy by suggesting that the higher the claw-marks on a tree the larger the jaguar, and therefore the more imprudent for any smaller jaguar to venture into such a territory on finding that he cannot measure up to the standard. It is, in fact, well established that cats indicate their territorial boundaries by spraying the undergrowth with their urine.

In their anti-social relations jaguars resemble tigers rather than lions, though (as in the case of the tiger) there is some evidence that in the remoter parts of their range they may sometimes associate in small 'prides', composed no doubt of immature beasts led perhaps by a barren female. However, there is no confirmation of Eduardo Prado's assertion that adult jaguars, in contrast to pumas, almost invariably associate in parties of one male and two females; and that while one of the latter remains in the den to look after the cubs, the male and the other female go out hunting. As an instance of such an association he refers to an occasion when he was called out to shoot a 'pair of tigers', whose presence had stopped all work by a road construction gang some thirty miles outside Manaos, despite the lack of any evidence that they were man-eaters. He eventually located their lair in a pile of rocks, from which came the characteristic stench of putrid flesh and old bones. At daylight the next morning tracks indicated that the jaguars had recently returned to the lair, dragging a stag; and on his companion slipping and snapping a branch, two jaguars emerged, followed by a third when an explosive was thrown into the den.

Since Prado's name will be cropping up from time to time his credentials had better be established here and now. Born and bred in Manaos, he was an experienced explorer and hunter, though a dubious naturalist, and was Hamilton Rice's guide in 1924 to the country of the Macuxi and Xiriana Indians on the Rio Branco, and also took part in one of the searches for Raymond Maufrais—that unhappy, deluded young Frenchman who, in order apparently to prove to himself that he was not a coward, persisted in adventuring on various expeditions, virtually without equipment, into the most inaccessible South American jungles, ultimately disappearing without trace in 1950 in the forests of the Tumuc-Humac Mountains in French Guiana.

In *The Lure of the Amazon*, Prado not only described the Blond Indians of the Sucurundi, but finally upgraded the Yeomiabas Amazons from myth to fact by staying with them for some days on the shores of Lake Yacura (twenty days up the Nhamunda from Obidos) during their annual rendezvous with the men of one of the various tribes that visited them in rota. It may be remembered that it was about the year 1640 that Teixeira, one of the Portuguese founders of Belem, was told by the Tupinamba Indians that there were Amazons near the Rio Cunuri, some twenty-six leagues below their most outlying settlement,

The southern region of South America

and that they met by arrangement with warriors of the Guacara tribe at Mt Yacambia.

But, to return to jaguars, the general opinion is that they are gregarious only during the love season, as Azara put it, when the males congregate eight or sometimes more together. 'For days together we did not hear either jaguars or pumas in the forests,' wrote Paul Fountain on the Purus in north-west Brazil. 'Then the whole night through they would be heard calling each other. The noise they sometimes make is terrific—or appears to be in these great solitudes, where there is generally the silence of death. At the pairing time both jaguars and pumas squall most abominably. They are not gregarious, but sometimes, as at this spot, a very large number of animals congregate within a small area. We met with twenty jaguars here to one puma, and I am sure that we might have killed over a hundred in a few days.'

Fountain would seem to have been an exceptionally observant amateur naturalist, though prone to generalisations. He was also an explorer extraordinary, in as much as over a period of more than thirty years after the American Civil War he explored extensive areas of both North and South America (as a pedlar and collector of birds) with one leg in irons. He is apparently the only man to have left a record of jaguars mating, in his description of the largest he ever shot. This was a female with a magnificent pelage (like most females) being courted by a gaunt and lanky old male on the shores of a lake on the Purus:

> She received him very spitefully, several times clawing him so severely that the fur flew from him in a small cloud. He took his punishment very chivalrously, retreating humbly, and waiting some minutes before making another advance, the female growling savagely as he approached. When I shot her the male gave a startled glance in my direction, and then rushed up a tree to a height of sixty feet.

Outside the mating season jaguars roar mainly when hunting at night and especially, it is said, prior to bad weather, as howler monkeys do. A hunting jaguar also talks to itself through the

B

forest, as a tiger does, with deep far-carrying throaty grunts; and purrs continually in pleasurable anticipation when circling a camp or cattle-pen, or if impatient with hunger snarls and growls with a menacing hoarse coughing *uh, uh, uh*. To George Cherrie, the appalling power of a jaguar's roaring, composed of five, six or a dozen repetitions of that short, sharp guttural *uh*, accelerating and crescending, was a more terrifying sound than the roaring of lions; while to Charles Waterton, who heard continual roaring every night from jaguars on the Essequibo, in sudden bursts that echoed among the hills like thunder, it resembled the roar of the caiman. That this was not a fanciful analogy is confirmed by William Beebe, who compared the latter's 'suppressed sighs' to the terminal roars of a lion's cadence.

In the tropics, jaguars breed in almost any month of the year (as they do in captivity), and Fountain saw cubs of all sizes on the Purus. Towards the extremes of their range, however, the young are born in the spring (reputedly as early as January in northern Mexico and the USA); but our knowledge of their breeding habits in the wild is mainly conjectural. The females are believed to litter in alternate years, after 100 days' gestation (93–95 days in captivity), and produce from one to four cubs. A captive female, when a little over three years old, gave birth to one cub on 10 November and, after mating again between 23 December and 3 January, a second litter of three on 11 April; but such a timetable would not be feasible in the wild state, when prey must be killed for the cubs for many months. These cubs, which were 16in long at birth and weighed 12lb, were furred with a long woolly pale-buff pelage, heavily marked with rounded black spots (with faint indications of pale centres) and narrow black facial stripes.

The cubs are reported to spend six weeks in the den, sometimes a cave or ruined temple or citadel, and to remain with their mother for one or possibly two years. By the latter age they are sexually mature though not more than 170lb in weight, and able to fend for themselves. This ability is confirmed by the Jivaro Indians of northern Peru who, believing like many Indian peoples that eminent chiefs and *shamans* can be transformed after death into jaguars, supply the body of a dead chief with food every month over a period of two years, after which a young jaguar can kill for itself.

When fully grown, an average-sized male jaguar measures 6ft in length (the female a fifth less) plus 20 to 30in of relatively short tail, and stands between 27 and 30in at the shoulder. There are very few records of jaguars exceeding a total length of 9ft. They are, therefore, rather smaller than tigers and weigh considerably less, since a good-sized male reaches a weight of only 250lb (and a female only 200lb) in comparison with a tiger's 400lb. Although these weights are seldom reached by jaguars in such parts of their range as Mexico, very much heavier specimens have been recorded in Amazonia and the Mato Grosso, particularly on the upper Paraguay where, in Roosevelt's opinion, the average female jaguar was heavier and more powerful than a male puma or an African leopard, and with her big bones and great girth, heavy chest and strongly-muscled forelegs, presented the same appearance of strength as a lion or tiger; while a large male proved to be very nearly double the weight of any African male leopards he had shot, and almost the weight of a small lioness. Jaguars on the Perene in northern Peru are reported to be very large, and Colonel Leonard Clark (the swashbuckling USA intelligence officer *cum* explorer extraordinary who was drowned in a Venezuelan river in 1957) put up a jaguar, which he estimated to have weighed 350lb, when hunting with dogs on the Perene. To be more specific, a jaguar of 308lb was shot after breaking the neck of a bullock on a ranch in the Peruvian *montana*, and a companion of Clark shot another of 315lb in the Quintana Roo; while Sacha Siemel, the Latvian-born hunter who killed more than three hundred cattle-eating jaguars in the swampy Xarayes country in the north-west of the Mato Grosso, recorded weights of more than 350lb.

Although the smallest known jaguars inhabit Mexico, it is impossible to build up any geographical cline or regular grading of size by locality. From the 101 specimens they examined, Nelson and Goldman listed sixteen possible races: but found that though one region, such as the Campeche in Yucatan, might be inhabited by a small race, much larger jaguars were to be found in neighbouring regions such as Vera Cruz and Tabasca.

The jaguar's pelage of short, rather bristly hair varies from clear yellow (whitish on the belly) to tawny. Possibly this variation is associated with habitat, for Caspar Whitney noted that all the jaguars he saw and shot on the Venezuelan plains were paler coloured than those in heavily forested country. The ground colour is overlaid with heavily-spotted black or dark-brown rosettes or irregularly shaped blotches (faintly visible on the glossy satin pelt of a black jaguar). The rosettes tend to concentrate into black bars along the spine and on the chest and throat, into solid ovals on the legs, into irregular spots on the belly, and into rings around the lower half of the tail. Although a jaguar's rosettes are fewer and larger than a leopard's and and spotted within, it is not always possible to differentiate between their pelts; and Schomburgk noted that out of several hundred skins used as hunting-bags by the Maripa Indians, only two or three bore a similar pattern, while only rarely did the pattern of skin resemble that on the other side. Although the face is unstriped, the backs of the ears are black, and lack the white 'flash' characteristic of the tiger's.

Melanism is much commoner among jaguars than among any of the other large cats, and appears to be a dominant character: whereas in leopards it is recessive. Black and spotted cubs occur in the same litter, and although Jacob von Tschudi found the black variety more numerous in the lower river jungles than in the higher forests, and Schomburgk saw only two black skins among several hundred he examined from the rain-forests of British Guiana, it seems unlikely that the incidence of melanism is influenced by environmental factors. There are, in fact, a number of records indicating that black jaguars may be as common as, or even outnumber, spotted jaguars in the drier regions of north-eastern Brazil.

2

The Hunting Jaguar

There are, of course, certain climatic and physical factors that predators cannot ignore. We have seen, for example, that jaguars are generally reported to be much more numerous in the Mato Grosso than in Amazonia. The obvious reason for this is that neither predator nor prey can live permanently in those vast areas of the Amazon jungle that are flooded to a depth of 50ft during a rainy season which endures for upwards of half of every year, and when as much as 30in of rain may fall in twenty-four hours:

> The forest is one vast inchoate roaring of rain on leaves: solid walls of vitreous grey water which hang or sway to and fro in the air— [wrote Emil Egli, who accompanied the photographer Emil Schulthess on his expedition to the Amazon some ten years ago.]
>
> The water moves onward from day to day. Nothing stands in its way any longer: the land is absolutely flat. Thousands upon thousands of square miles go under. The water pushes ahead for so long as the rain and the tributaries can move it. And as there is practically no gradient to take it off, the water remains on the land it has seized. The forest rises from the watery desolation like gigantic growths of seaweed.

That experienced explorer, G. M. MacCreagh, was amazed at the almost total absence of animal life on the Rio Negro after the annual floods had subsided:

> Moist and steamy and dim-lit it is, under that impenetrable canopy of trees and interlaced vines through which the sun can never reach down; soggy ground fit only for sluggish caimans and water-monitors and huge snakes. A gloomy, menacing silence

hangs heavily on the hot greenhouse air, broken only when rank fruit drops with a soft *plosh* into the muck.

This perennial flooding or *ygapo* of thousands of square miles of Amazonia, and the colossal subsidences of river banks and the forest itself, must effect, seasonally or permanently, immense alterations in the distribution of all animal life. Some jaguars, and also pumas, voyage for many miles down the flooded rivers on the trunks of trees, but the majority migrate to higher ground and especially to islands. Nearly all jaguar trails lead to rivers, and it is islands, rivers, marsh and swamp that are the normal haunts of jaguars in country less subject to flooding, because these are also the haunts of their prey. Dense jungle is as unsuitable environmentally for game as it is for men. Even Indians, in Fountain's experience, are unable to penetrate more than a hundred yards into parts of the Mato Grosso forest, where 'the trees are literally matted together, forming a forest wall, which makes as firm a barrier as one of masonry would be. I have travelled about 130 miles along the outskirts of such a district, and been unable to penetrate anywhere, or by any means, except the watercourses. These I have ascended as far as possible, finding the forest on each side as dense as on the outskirts.'

By contrast, there are also in both Amazonia and the Mato Grosso great areas of open woodland no denser than an English parkland, as Fountain found when he reached a hilly tributary of the otherwise very flat Purus in Brazil. This tributary swarmed with game (including a hundred or more tapirs), with the result that both jaguars and pumas were very abundant. It was in the upper Purus country that he discovered a lake, some nine miles long by five in width, with five islands. The shores were frequented by countless deer, and jaguars living on the islands had trodden regular paths to their favourite landing places:

> On one morning that was spent here we saw eleven land from one island alone in the course of an hour. This was in the early morning, and their object in leaving their lairs seemed to be to

feast on prey killed the previous evening. Before ten o'clock several of them were seen to swim back to the island, doubtless to spend the greater part of the day in sleep, though the jaguar is here not so nocturnal as it is in some other parts of the country. There were a few jaguars on the move in this district at all hours of the day; while, as soon as it was dark, they swarmed to a dangerous extent, moving about fearlessly in all directions.

Leopold found that Mexican jaguars were almost exclusively nocturnal and rarely seen abroad during the day, when they rested in the seclusion of thick brush or rocks. 'At the edge of the Araguaya jungle, on the sand, thickly dappled with tracks, some of them fresh since the night before, you looked first for those of jaguars,' wrote Peter Fleming, 'suave round cups in the sand, each very neatly straight behind the other, like a cat's tracks in the snow.' A jaguar's relatively short, rounded head is almost as flexible as an owl's, and his binocular vision enables him to focus on his prey precisely: whereas the eyes of deer, peccaries and tapir are set wide apart in order to cover as large a field of vision as possible, and such prey have difficulty in determining the identity of a motionless object, as every deer-stalker knows. Yves Manciet, the French photographer, was so impressed with the extraordinary eyes of jaguars—enormous gold-flecked eyes, especially golden against a black pelt, and capable of looking at man calmly and without hate—that he never shot another after his first. But Fountain's experiences emphasize what is almost certainly true of most predators and prey alike—that they are exclusively or mainly nocturnal only where persecuted by man. The animals on the Purus were so tame that he presumed that they had not even been disturbed by Indians; and he was particularly impressed by the jaguars: 'One slunk by me like a great dog, within twenty yards. He was probably gorged, for he moved slowly down to the lake, and swam off to one of the islands. This was not the only occasion on which a jaguar or puma passed unpleasantly close to one or other of us; but in no case did they seem inclined to attack.'

There are many descriptions of diurnal encounters with

jaguars, especially near rivers, where they are most frequently seen and at their most relaxed:

> During our passage down the Esmeraldas [wrote W. R. Stevenson almost one hundred and fifty years ago] I was very much delighted by the sight of a full-grown tiger, which lay basking in the sun on a sand-bank that projected from the side of the river almost across it. The noble brute was stretched close to the bank, frequently dipping his tail into the water, and sprinkling it over him, while his muzzle and feet touched the stream. After watching the animal for a quarter of an hour, my palanqueros became impatient, and at last taking their lances they jumped ashore from the canoe, but at the same moment the tiger sprang to his feet, yawned, stretched himself, and trotted into the woods.

On the Essequibo, fifty years later, C. B. Brown encountered one large jaguar sitting on the river bank, gazing down on his canoe; a second lying on a flat rock sunning itself, ears flicking the flies away; and a third lying full-length on a sloping log, of which one end was in the water and the other on the bank. As the canoe approached to within ten yards of the bank, the third animal began to work its claws on the log like a cat, but did not retreat.

To a jaguar a boat, whether manned or empty, is a harmless object on the water that can sometimes be used as transport—as in the case of a Guiana jaguar which swam out to a lumber barge and, to the discomfiture of its occupants, clambered aboard by means of a projecting plank. This recalls Rolf Blomberg's tale of two hunters who were paddling downstream in their canoe when they caught sight of a jaguar crossing the river. On being fired at the jaguar swam directly for the canoe and heaved himself into it. Exit hunters head-first into the river. By the time they had waded ashore the canoe was disappearing round a bend with the jaguar sitting in it licking himself, as 'pleased as Punch'. Again, a jaguar is forcing its way across a swiftly flowing river in the Mato Grosso at sunset. It does not turn its massive head when Julian Duguid starts the engine of his launch, nor alter course when the launch is about to intercept it, even when six shots spurt up gouts of water around it. A seventh bullet strikes its neck; but when the boat is within a few inches of the shore, its prow almost touching the jaguar (now treading water), the latter suddenly finds purchase on a sunken tree and leaps into the forest so swiftly that another bullet misses. The only reminder of the encounter is a stale and musky odour about the bushes and in the air.

Nicholas Guppy was given a similar account of a jaguar's extraordinary ability to leap out of deep water. When he was camping one night in a British Guiana jungle a jaguar had roared at some distance, and subsequently gnashed and cracked its teeth on the opposite side of the river. His guide, who was much excited, then described how on one occasion when he and his brother had been in a boat, they had come upon a jaguar feeding on a caiman. On seeing them the jaguar swam off into very deep water. Determining to run it down and crush it against the rocky river bank, one brother raced the engine to get up speed, while the other shot an arrow into the jaguar's side; but just as the boat was about to hit it, the jaguar leapt right out of the water on to the top of the bank some twelve feet above. On Guppy suggesting that the jaguar must have taken off from a submerged rock, the guide was emphatic that this had not been the case, because nowhere could they reach the bottom with a pole.

Leopold considered that in the tropical forests of the new world the large cats are the only predators capable of controlling the populations of hoofed game such as deer, peccaries and tapir, and take over completely the ecological function performed in part by the wolf and coyote in temperate zones. But in South America the numbers of prey must be relatively insignificant in comparison with the vast areas of forest, marsh and savanna they inhabit; and it was Fountain's opinion that the prey of jaguars consisted largely of very small animals such as rodents (including rats and mice) and such birds as quails and tinamus, and post-mortems conducted by Ferreira revealed that mice, lizards, snakes, rabbits, agoutis, monkeys and sloths, small birds, parrots and wild turkeys had all been taken by the Mexican jaguars he shot. All cats eat a certain amount of vegetable food, and just as the Indian tiger is ravished by the pungent and aromatic fruit of the *Careya arborea*, so the jaguar, according to Spruce, prefers the alligator pear (the laurel *Persea gratissima*) to all other foods; though the only confirmation of this preference would appear to be the statement by an Indian that in the Brazilian forest between Uaupas and Japura he had come upon four jaguars growling and snarling over the fruits lying beneath an alligator pear.

Before the advent of Europeans with their horses and cattle, the jaguar's main prey must have been wild pig (in the form of peccaries), deer, and tapir—as was the case with the tiger in Asia. His only predatory rival was the puma, as the leopard was the tiger's. Although the puma ranges right through the jaguar's habitat, and far beyond its marches both to the north and to the south, it is primarily a predator of the pampas and mountains rather than of the jungle. Nevertheless, from the records of skins obtained in the southern Mato Grosso, F. W. Miller judged the ratio of jaguars to pumas to be little higher than two to one in that region. But although both can be found in the same jungle one must presume that, as in the case of the more closely associated tiger and leopard, they do not compete significantly for prey and living space; for were this the case, one or other would have been drastically reduced in numbers or driven to the extremities of its range. Nor would one expect them to interbreed, though Sacha Siemel shot what he believed to be a jaguar–puma hybrid in the Mato Grosso. He described it to Duguid as being a heavily built, fawn-coloured animal with brown spots and a dark stripe along the spine. In captivity, jaguars have mated with both leopards and lions, and have produced young.

However, when one takes into account the immense range available to both jaguars and pumas, it is possible that the numbers of pumas on the pampas have been as potent a factor in preventing the permanent colonization of these by jaguars as the paucity of the jaguar's favoured prey and the unfavourable terrain. All the same it is surprising to find B. S. Wright stating that pumas compete directly with jaguars for food, and that the two give each other a wide berth when on the same range. Indians of the central and northern parts of South America state that the two fight to the death whenever they meet, with the puma the killer in most instances despite its weight disadvantage. Although the measurements and weights of jaguars and pumas overlap, with those pumas in the south of their range much larger than those in the tropics, where they compete most directly with jaguars, the latter are considerably more massive. W. H. Hudson also asserted that pumas, being much the swifter and more agile, persistently persecuted jaguars: moving about them with such rapidity as to confuse them and, when an opportunity occurred, springing upon their backs and inflicting severe wounds with teeth and claws. Jaguars with scarred backs or with severe wounds are frequently shot, and there is at least one record (in northern California) of a puma killing such a formidable beast as a grizzly, four or five times its own weight. Fountain, however, witnessed a jaguar so maul a puma almost its equal in size that he thought it unlikely to recover from its wounds.

A major difficulty in writing a natural history of the jaguar has been that of assessing the worth and probity of information obtained from the old naturalists and explorers. One has great respect for these pioneers: but even naturalists with international reputations such as Darwin, Alexander von Humboldt or Schomburgk, accepted in good faith a great deal of hearsay evidence, which they were unable to check from personal experience; while Hudson has been castigated as having no first-hand knowledge whatever of either jaguars or pumas.

Peccaries, deer, tapirs—these the jaguar stalks, or waits for in ambush at a water-hole, beside a game-trail, or on the limb of an overhanging tree. In view of the fact that a jaguar, when excited, emits a glandular secretion with an odour strong enough to be detected by Leonard Clark's Peruvian guide at a distance of 50ft, a tree ambush would afford obvious advantages. Clark himself, when trailing a jaguar, 50yd in from the edge of an Everglades-type swamp, was suddenly aware of a fearful stench, recalling the acrid smell of tigers' and leopards' cages in a circus. On turning round slowly and cautiously, he saw a jaguar crouching motionless 15yd distant, only partly concealed behind a short clump of grass, with its flat head and hindquarters plainly visible. Its hind feet were drawn forward under and alongside its belly, all set to spring. In the setting sun its tawny hide shone as brightly as if painted with hollow black rosettes.

Manciet had a similar experience when his Brazilian hunter took him to a clearing of grass several feet high beside a tributary of the Madeira. This clearing, according to the hunter, was a gathering place for *oncas*, to which they resorted to warm themselves on sunny days. After waiting for more than two hours, some 20yd downwind of the clearing, the hunter announced that he could smell a jaguar. On their right the grass stirred slightly at the silent approach of an animal, and an instant later it parted and the *onca* appeared. He stopped once or twice to snuff at the air, but suddenly caught their scent and whipped round to face them, with his back slightly arched, growling softly.

'Jaguar' is perhaps a French adaptation or mutilation of the Guiana Indian *Yaouar*: but could equally well be derived from *Jaguara*—he who strikes down his prey with a single bound. The lightning bound and strike are, of course, preceded by the infinitely careful slow stalk, during the course of which the constant twitching of the tip of the jaguar's tail, far removed from its body, may perhaps distract the prey's attention from the body inching its way forward, belly to ground. Manciet himself experienced a certain fascination in watching the spasmodic lashings of a jaguar's tail against its flanks, and the Indians told him that a jaguar was capable of luring his prey towards him by that hypnotic swishing of the tail. Other Indian tribes claim that a jaguar can imitate the call of almost any beast (or bird) in order to attract it. This is not necessarily folklore, since there is considerable evidence that tigers can, and do, imitate various species of deer for this purpose.

If the stalk is successful then, in the words of Emil Schulthess' guide Sergio, who had taken part in several Amazon expeditions, the 'jaguar rears up on both hind legs before pouncing on its prey'; and he also gave us to understand that the *onca* attacks only if he can see his victim's head. If unsuccessful, which must often be the case, then the pursuit of this particular prey is abandoned for, unlike the puma, a jaguar very rarely attempts to kill more than one animal in a herd. As Fountain puts it in his refreshingly naïve way:

> Both pumas and jaguars often have to go without food for lengthened periods, for not only are their victims as wily as they are, but often escape the jaguar's attack. It is quite as much as the latter can do to pull down a full-grown tapir, while with the horse or cow he often finds he has caught a tartar.

As to the actual method of killing, Fountain goes on to say:

> Both jaguars and pumas kill large game, generally, by breaking the neck; but I do not think this is done in the manner which is generally thought. I have watched them very carefully, and my opinion is that the neck is broken by a quick blow of the paw. All cats strike freely with their paws, but they cannot do so without unsheathing their claws, which become imbedded in the flesh. It is the motion of disengaging the claws which has misled the observers and induced them to think that the jaguar or puma was endeavouring to break the victim's neck by drawing back the head. Both jaguars and pumas sometimes kill their larger victims by simply tearing out the throat without breaking the bones of the neck.

It was Schomburgk's experience that, after first sucking blood from its prey (cattle), a jaguar would gulp down 10 or 15lb of flesh from the breast and neck, before dragging the remainder of the carcass to cover under the nearest bush; and according to Fountain, neither jaguars nor pumas crack the bones of their prey in order to get at the marrow, as bears or wolves do, but lick every scrap of flesh off the bones with their rough tongues. A big cat's teeth are essentially killing and rending tools, not grinders. Six of the ninety-two skulls examined by Nelson and Goldman had one or more canines broken; and in one case, that of an adult male, all the canines had been broken off short and worn down to smooth stubs.

Humboldt observed that a jaguar would often stay beside its kill for a considerable period, possibly for some days if it was a large beast, alternately eating and sleeping. But some jaguars never return to the remains of a kill after the first feed. Stevenson, indeed, went so far as to state that, after killing a bullock or colt on the savanna, a jaguar would not return to the same locality for some months.

All the big cats are incredibly strong, and a jaguar's strength is demonstrated by his ability to drag his kill great distances, particularly if it has been made at some distance from cover. Leopold refers to carcasses weighing more than 200kg (440lb) being dragged 2–3km; Roosevelt, to a horse being dragged more than a mile; and Azara, to an instance of a jaguar which, after crossing a broad deep river, seized a horse, dragged it 60yd or so across ploughed land, and finally re-crossed the river with it. According to Colonel Fawcett, jaguars also kill and drag ashore manatees, despite the fact that those on the Amazon, while averaging only 7 or 8ft in length, may reach 15ft and weigh 1,000lb or more.

Whether he does, or does not, return to his kill will no doubt depend upon how much interference a particular jaguar has been subjected to by man or pumas—or even wolves, for there is an old record of some Texas Rangers coming upon a jaguar feeding upon a mustang, encircled by eight or ten waiting wolves. If it is his intention to return to the kill, then he will hide the remains in the bush, or cover them with sticks, grass, weeds and earth, to conceal them from the sharp eyes of such avian scavengers as *krakras* which are abroad in search of carrion before daylight, or vultures which begin their search at dawn. The common black vultures are quick to locate kills, and a flock in a tree is an almost certain sign that a jaguar is lying beside its kill. Von Humboldt saw one jaguar, lying under a *zamany* tree with a capybara under one paw, surrounded by vultures. On his boat approaching, the jaguar drew back into cover and the vultures moved in on the kill: whereupon the jaguar leaped into the middle of them and, in a fit of rage, expressed by his gait and the movements of his tail, carried off his prey into the forest.

3

Jaguars and their Prey

Paul Fountain describes how small deer came at night in great numbers to drink at the Purus lake, where the jaguars lay in wait for them:

The deer swam gracefully and well, both in the river and in the lake. On one occasion we saw two jaguars attempt to intercept some of them that were swimming towards the bank of the lake. The deer saw them and changed their direction, and though the jaguars galloped round the lake the deer were too quick for them and escaped. The jaguars seemed to be aware that they would have no chance of overtaking the deer in the water, the latter swimming with much greater speed than the cats.

Of all the cats, the jaguar is most at home in the water, roaming at night across the marshes and swamps so typical of the Mato Grosso, and along the banks of *bayous* and ponds, or straight through them when in pursuit of swamp deer. He does not hesitate to cross any broad stream he encounters when hunting, and swims with ease over the widest river with the tip of his erected tail bent above the surface; whereas the puma swims slowly and awkwardly.

There are extraordinarily few references to jaguars hunting deer, or to the deer themselves for that matter, though Roosevelt observed that in the Taquari marshes the jaguars hunted peccaries more habitually than the swamp deer, despite this deer's red coat being vividly obvious against the green marshes, while the black of its erected tail, when it turned to flee, was additionally revealing. He added that there was nothing in the swamp deer's habitat with which red harmonised.

Of the tapir and its relations with the jaguar we know rather more. Though widely distributed, tapirs are generally reported as nowhere abundant, living a solitary nocturnal life in the dense cover of undisturbed rain-forest, rarely being seen in pairs. But our knowledge of the habits of the South American fauna is minimal, because so few of the explorers of its forests have been field naturalists. The best that we can do, therefore, is to attempt to read between the lines of their accounts. Although Fountain, as already noted, encountered as many as a hundred tapirs in one locality on the Purus, this was an exceptional concentration, and only rarely did he come upon even five or six together. He observed that they loved to lie among tall rushes, close to dense forest, wallowing for hours in the mud; and were often seen completely enveloped in a dry coat of mud, possibly as a defence against the attacks of insects, possibly for cooling purposes. Algot Lange, indeed, states that, in order to survive, a tapir must be able to spend several hours a day partially immersed in ooze, and that it can plough through mud that would engulf any other animal. However, Henry Rusby, who botanised in various regions of the Americas from New Mexico southwards over a period of forty years, observed that on the Beni, in Bolivia, tapirs were tormented by biting flies settling in clouds about their eyes, ears, nose and mouth—their only vulnerable parts; and that they were unable to escape these attacks by taking to the water because the flies renewed their attacks whenever the tapirs surfaced. When a tapir was in the forest, these flies were preyed upon, according to his Indian hunter, by the *llama-anta* (the tapir-caller): a bird resembling a small hawk, whose call is almost an exact imitation of the tapir's 'squeal'.

In Peru, after resting up during the day in the humid forest, numbers of tapirs emerge in the cool evening to break into the fields of coca, to the low-growing leaves of which they are very partial. Since they also feed on mandioca and most leaves and fruits, including the prickly leaves of the young shoots of javary palms, they do much damage to the fields of the Indians in some regions. From the Indians at Serra on the Rio Negro, Alfred Russell Wallace collected a delightful fragment of folklore.

Page 33 Jaguar and black mate

Page 34 An Amazonian jaguar in its typical environment, riverine jungle and swamp

Tapirs, like peccaries, are in the habit of dropping their horse-like dung in one place: but according to these Serra Indians they drop their dung only in water. However, if there is no water in the vicinity, the tapir fashions a rough basket from leaves and carries its dung to the nearest stream. It was in these circumstances that one tapir met another in the forest with its basket in its mouth: 'What have you in the basket?' said the one. 'Fruit,' answered the other. 'Let me have some,' said the first. 'I won't,' said the other; upon which the first tapir pulled the basket from the other's mouth and broke it open. On seeing its contents both turned tail, ashamed, and ran away in opposite directions, never to go near that place again during the remainder of their lives.

Tapirs are usually described as shy and timid, but in some localities where not persecuted they can become comparatively tame. Fawcett found all the animals very confident above Yorongas, then the last rubber post on the lower Amazon, with even a tapir standing its ground and watching his boat with mild curiosity. So too, F. W. Up de Graff noted that since Yacu-Mammam, one of the Jivaro Indians' two gods, possessed the power of changing from a tapir into an anaconda and finally into a frog, these three creatures were never molested by the Indians for fear of the god's anger; and to this fact he attributed the tameness of tapirs throughout the Jivaros' country. But though, as we have seen, Fountain also found the wildlife to be extremely tame on the virtually uninhabited Purus—the only locality in which monkeys would descend as low as 30 or 40ft to look at him—the tapirs were as timid as he had always known them to be, despite the fact that they were abroad at all hours of the day.

Opinions differ as to the acuteness of the tapir's senses. When Hyatt Verrill, an experienced explorer who passed much of thirty years in the jungles of central and northern South America, stated that it has keener eyesight and sharper ears than any other animal in the jungle, he was clearly indulging in generalities. A hunter walking upwind can approach to within a few yards of one, and a jaguar certainly closer; while Thomas Bigg-

c

Wither describes watching a tapir strolling across a sandbank to take its morning bathe in the river, where it rolled and dived and snorted, unaware of his crew's presence not a dozen feet distant. Despite its great weight of up to 750lb a tapir moves quietly, though imprinting deeply punched tracks not unlike those of a small elephant, but with the three toes on the forefoot and the four on the hindfoot widely splayed; and in Verrill's experience can travel rapidly and noiselessly through the thickest jungle. He cites an instance of sitting on a log waiting for a tapir he had been tracking to be driven up to him, when it suddenly emerged without a sound from the cane-brake only 6ft from him: 'His little red-rimmed pig-like eyes gleamed viciously, his proboscis was drawn up and wrinkled, exposing yellow ugly-looking teeth, and the ridge of stiff hair on his neck fairly bristling with anger.'

Gordon MacCreagh is on the Bopi river, a tributary of the upper Beni:

> In the sand by the edge of this hidden creek is a curious triple-toed trail, the fresh tracks of a big tapir which has sauntered along not later than last night. The tracks show where the beast has suddenly halted and stood looking at something in the shadows of the underbush. It is written clearly how the tapir then wheeled and trotted back the way he had come; how the trot broke into a frenzied gallop.
>
> And there in the underbush, where the tapir had looked, are the marks of four great padded paws, the nail-tips showing where the forepaws had tensed and flexed in excitement. Then, overlaying the galloping triple toes, the widespread pads of a great jaguar, clearing twenty feet at a bound.

A tapir has no physical powers of defence against any large predator, though it may try to knock down and bite and stamp on a man, and MacCreagh was chased by a bull which he had stung with small shot. Therefore it must employ various protective devices against attacks by jaguars. In Honduras, where both tapirs and jaguars are, or were, common, the former lie up in the densest thickets of bamboo or prickly thorn which, though alien to their preference for open swampy country, afford them some protection against jaguars which are in the habit of stalking them while they are sleeping and springing upon their backs. However, should a tapir be surprised in this way, it is not necessarily easy prey. The jaguar must strike to kill instantly. If he delays or fails to penetrate a vital artery, the tapir plunges blindly through bush and forest, bursting a way through by by sheer bulk and strength and, more often than not, brushing the jaguar off its back against trees and branches, before its thick hide has been fatally penetrated by the jaguar's canines.

When Lange was camping in the Javari jungle, he was awakened in the early hours of the morning by a terrific roaring:

> Sitting up and staring fearfully into the darkness, I heard the crashing of under-brush and trees close upon us. My first thought was of a hurricane. The noise grew louder and more terrifying. Suddenly the little world around me went smash in one mad upheaval. The roof of the *tambo* collapsed and fell upon us. At the same instant I felt some huge body brush past me, but the object passed swiftly in the direction of the creek.
>
> Someone now thought of striking a light to discover the extent of the damage. The *tambo* was a wreck; the hammocks were one tangled mass. Jerome followed the 'hurricane' to the creek and soon solved the mystery. It was a jaguar, which had sprung upon the back of a large tapir while the animal was feeding in the woods behind our *tambo*. The tapir started for the creek in the hope of knocking the jaguar off its back by rushing through the under-brush; not succeeding in this, its next hope was the water in the creek. It had chosen a straight course through our *tambo*.

No doubt jaguars kill many young tapirs, which are born in the summer and accompany their mothers for the first year or so. 'The cows seemed exceedingly jealous of letting the calf away from their sides, and the cow never has the male with her when she has a young calf,' noted the ever-observant Fountain; and he also implies that a cow may sometimes be accompanied by more than one calf.

The Indians on the Araguaya, where Everard Im Thurn found

jaguars numerous, differentiated between the ordinary spotted jaguars that preyed mainly on peccaries, and the black jaguars preying mainly on tapirs: just as it is the latter that are reported to prey most extensively on turtles on the Rio Negro sandbanks. Such distinctions do not commend themselves as good natural history: but so often in researching into the habits of the big mammals one has come across some discredited item of native lore which has subsequently proved to be true, or to have been garbled in transference to the hunter or explorer.

A tapir's last line of defence is the water, which is its second home—so much so that out of twenty-eight tapirs shot by Bigg-Wither's party during the course of eighteen months on the Parana only two were killed on shore. One of its favourite foods is the coarse, fleshy 'pacu-grass' (*Podostemonacae*) that grows in luxuriant clumps on the rocks of rapids, forming useful cushions for boats negotiating them, which is also eaten by large shoals of the red, gold, purple, dark-blue or black pacu fish, that propel their 10lb disc-shaped bodies into the shallows and graze the clumps while lying on their sides. Tapirs may not be able to run along the river-bed as Fountain stated that he had observed them to do; but there is no reason to suppose that they cannot walk on the bottom as the Malayan tapir does, and they can certainly travel considerable distances under water. One will usually allow a canoe to approach to within 30 or 40yd before diving for a minute or two, after first closing its nostrils and retracting its flexible proboscis beneath its upper lip. Bigg-Wither refers to a wounded tapir that swam 200 yd under water to the river bank and made its way into the forest—though on one of his canoemen barking like a hunting dog, the tapir came rushing back to the river again. Another, wounded when a mile from the shore of the Essequibo, was timed by William Beebe to stay down for a period of five minutes; while according to Lange, a tapir can travel for fifteen minutes below the surface of a swamp and emerge 100yd distant without leaving any trace of air-bubbles because of the heavy consistency of the ooze.

One presumes that the jaguar's favourite prey is, as in the case of the tiger, wild pig. These are represented in South America by the two species of peccary, though they are not true pigs. The most numerous is the smaller collared peccary (the *javelina* or *jabali*), standing under 2ft at the shoulder and weighing from 30 to 65lb. The javelinas range right through the jaguar's country from the southern states of the USA to the La Plata, and although their natural environment is forest they also inhabit the dense scrub of the northern desert lands and the scattered clumps of oak-trees on the Texan grasslands, providing that water is available in these habitats, together with retreats in which they can lie up during the midday heat and the night cold, whether these be caves, old burrows or hollow logs, roots at the bases of trees or even a giant ant-eater's 'earth'. They feed mainly in the early morning and late evening on roots and tubers, grubs, worms, snakes, berries, cactus fruits, mesquite and cat-claw beans, pine-nuts and acorns. During the dry summer months, when little green vegetation is available, the prickly-pear is especially sought after, and the stomach-lining of a peccary killed at this season may be as full of spines as a pin-cushion.

Throughout most of their range *javelinas* travel in small sounders that rarely contain more than a dozen or score of individuals, possibly because of persistent culling by men and jaguars, for the denser the population of peccaries in any particular region the larger their herds. Where herds of fifty or a hundred members are ranging in the same locality, these on scenting danger will coalesce, and Fountain encountered herds of four or five hundred *javelinas* on several occasions near the Fresco river in the Mato Grosso.

The white-lipped peccary (the *huangana*, or *kairui*) is considerably larger than the *javelina* and twice the weight, and also darker in colour with a white under-jaw and lower cheek. The *huanganas* range freely from central Mexico south to Paraguay, preferring dense tropical jungle rather than the scrub-forest favoured by the *javelinas*, and are extremely conservative in their choice of habitat, being reluctant to move out of their particular jungle even when persistently persecuted. They are omnivorous in the broadest sense of the term, for while roots, figs and palm-nuts may be their staple foods, Archie Carr describes them as being the scourge of all small animals in Costa Rica (including young turtles when they are hatching), virtually clearing the forest of these when they pass in herds of from twenty to a hundred or more. A. del Toro says that the herds are organised, with the yearlings in the forefront, followed by the sub-adults and then the large boars and the sows with piglets in the rear. The latter (usually twins in the tropics) are precocious enough to get to their feet and dodge about in the under-brush a few hours after birth, and to join the mixed herd when a day or two old; though they are often left behind, to 'freeze' in the undergrowth, if the herd panics.

They pass with a low eerie moaning and a constant threatening rattling of tusks that resembles the clicking of a thousand pairs of castanets, as their lower jaws vibrate with extraordinary rapidity: 'There is a vocal noise like the distant beat of drums, and the rustling of many feet through the leaves sounds like wind in the trees,' wrote Up de Graff in reference to such a herd. 'The strong acrid odour of the herd hangs in the air and on shrubs and overhanging branches long after the animals have passed, and can be smelt a full mile away.' Both peccaries possess a large oily gland, positioned on the mid-line of the back a few inches in front of the very short tail. When an individual is sexually excited, or alarmed, or angry, the long hair on the back is erected, exposing the gland, which emits an offensive musky odour; though one questions whether it is so offensive that, as Stevenson asserted, the individual emitting it rolls about and places its nose close to the ground, as if to avoid the stench, while its companions immediately desert it! The American biologist, Lyle Sowls, who has made a social study of *javelinas*, describes how, on the contrary, when two friendly animals meet, they face in opposite directions and, with sides touching, rub their necks and jowls rhythmically over each other's scent glands. Although a peccary's scenting powers are poor, the heavy residues of musk on rocks and trees suggest that it may also serve identification purposes and perhaps demarcate the boundaries of a herd's territory which, in the case of the *javelina*, may be no more than two miles in diameter.

One would suppose that deposits of such a powerful scent would attract every jaguar in the neighbourhood. However, although *javelinas* may be more or less defenceless against jaguars, and are also preyed upon by ocelots and, in the northern parts of their range, by wolves, *huanganas* are formidable prey, being insensately ferocious and deceptively agile. Nevertheless, every large herd of *huanganas* is reported to be followed at a discreet distance through the forest by a jaguar picking off stragglers. This generalisation can perhaps be attributed to Esse-quibo Indians, who say that a 'master' jaguar will follow one herd wherever it goes, killing when hungry any peccary a little distant from the herd. However, it seems true enough that no jaguar (or puma for that matter) will attempt to attack a herd of peccaries, but only a solitary individual or one at the end of a file. Leaping down from his ambush in a tree, the jaguar makes his kill, and then leaps up into the tree again, to wait until all the peccaries have passed on, before descending to eat at leisure. Sometimes, however, a jaguar will have been so careless as to select a tree in which he is not able to climb out of reach of the peccaries; and there are a number of records of jaguars being slashed and torn to pieces by an infuriated herd of *huanganas*— and also eaten *in toto* according to Up de Graff, who was a most experienced explorer with seven years' first-hand knowledge of the upper Amazon. Stevenson gives a quaint account of such an incident in the woods along the Esmeraldas in Ecuador, describing how he found the two hind-quarters of a full-grown jaguar suspended from the trunk of a tree by its claws, which were buried to the quick in the wood. All the fore-parts appeared to have been torn away, and fragments of them were scattered about the ground:

> The sight astonished me, and I was not less surprised at the account which I received from the natives. The jaguar, for the purpose of killing the *saino*, on which it feeds, rushes on one of a herd, strikes it, and then betakes itself to a tree, which it ascends, and fastening its hind claws into the tree, hangs down sufficiently low to be able

to strike the *saino* with its claws, which having effected in a moment it draws itself up again, to escape being hurt by the enemy. However, it appeared that in this case the jaguar had been incautious, and the *saino* had caught it by the paw, when the whole herd immediately attacked it, and tore as much of it to pieces as they could reach.

Should a jaguar be still more careless and attack a herd of *huanganas* without taking the precaution of first locating a suitable tree to which he can retreat if set upon by the herd, his chances of survival may be slight. An Englishman, who had been living in the Brazilian village of Sao Jeronymo since about 1834, recounted to Bigg-Wither how he and a companion were squatting round the fire one night at their camp between two rivers, when they suddenly heard at a little distance a tremendous uproar of grunting, squeaking and clacking of tusks:

Pigs, said we both. It was bright moonlight, and the sound came from the direction of a little open patch in the forest, such as frequently occur where pine trees grow. Snatching up our guns from the ground beside us, we crept cautiously towards the sounds which still continued, though with less uproar than at first, and we soon came to the edge of the little clearing. Standing upon the extreme summit of an ant-hillock about five feet from the ground was a jaguar, surrounded by a large drove of pigs, perhaps fifty or sixty in number, all in a state of furious rage, and vainly endeavouring to get at their enemy perched on the ant-hill. Meantime the jaguar, with his tail stuck well up into the air, and with all four legs close together, balancing himself on the point of the ant-hillock, kept pacing round uneasily first in one direction and then another, as the infuriated pigs threatened this side and that side. It was clear that the game could not long be carried on in this fashion; either the pigs would give up the siege as hopeless, or the jaguar would get tired of his uncomfortable position and make a dash to escape. The end however came in a manner we did not expect. In a moment of forgetfulness, the tiger allowed his tail, which he had hitherto been holding well up out of reach of his besiegers, to droop slightly. In a second the unlucky appendage was seized by the pigs, its owner was pulled down from his perch into their midst, and a terrible battle began. Every now and then we could see the big yellow body of the jaguar surge up above the seething mass of pigs, and his powerful forepaws striking out deadly blows to right and left, only to sink down again the next instant into the midst of his raging enemies. Presently the uproar began to subside; but the jaguar had not emerged from the crowd, and we could see him nowhere. After waiting some little time longer the herd of pigs began to disperse, and we walked into the clearing. Still no jaguar was to be seen, but no less than fourteen pigs were lying dead or dying upon the ground. Presently Lopez, stooping down, picked up a fragment of something, and holding it up said, 'Aqui o tigre.' 'Here's the tiger.' It was a bit of the jaguar's skin. He had literally been torn to pieces by the pigs, and his body devoured or carried away by them. Only a few fragments of skin and hair remained on the field of battle.

More recently, in *Back of Beyond*, Harold Noice has described a similar experience when he and two companions were resting in the upper Negro jungle. After a while they heard the sharp rattling of a herd of peccaries' champing teeth; and then suddenly a terrifying, coughing cry as a large jaguar leaped across the trail scarcely 20ft ahead of them and disappeared into the tangled undergrowth. He was followed immediately by the peccaries, in hot pursuit.

The jaguar then sprang out on to the trail again and, catching sight of the men, hesitated momentarily. He was instantly attacked and gored by a boar, and then by the rest of the herd.

In the meantime Noice and his companions had climbed the nearest tree, from the safety of which they saw the jaguar torn to pieces, though not before several of the peccaries had been ripped open, while others had been killed by their fellows in the fury of the fray.

On Noice subsequently shooting two of the herd the remainder charged his tree, causing the slender trunk to sway under their onslaught as they tore huge strips of bark from it; but they then lost interest and drifted away.

The actions of a herd of peccaries are unpredictable, and a *huangana* may be one of the very few wild animals that will charge a man on sight, without provocation. By some hunters it is indeed considered the most dangerous South American mammal: but the hunter often speaks from his experience of wounded animals. However, according to Fountain, even the small *javelinas* do not hesitate to attack man:

> When a herd is feeding in a tract of forest they often disperse over a considerable area, but they always reassemble when they have done feeding; and their hearing must be very acute, for if one gives an alarm, which he may do by a kind of squeal, or by gnashing his tusks, they assemble to his aid with remarkable speed, rushing together angrily, with their tusks rattling at a tremendous rate. You may see them standing quite still, their snouts raised to the level of their backs and all pointing the same way, apparently listening. Suddenly away they rush, full charge and all together. Then the hunter must tree for his life, and he will be fortunate if his foes keep him prisoner for twenty-four hours only; and if he commences firing from the shelter of his tree the peccaries will take cover, but will still wait hours for him.

No doubt the aggressiveness of a herd of *huanganas* has been exaggerated, and they certainly by no means always charge. Peccaries are short-sighted, and the panic veering-off of a startled herd must often have been mistaken for a charge. This is illustrated by Up de Graff's experience that an attacking herd, after being fired at from a tree, would sweep straight past the tree and continue running for several miles. Schomburgk, too, describes how, when his party were crossing a woody oasis on the Rupunini, they heard in the distance a peculiar noise exactly resembling the sound of hooves on the gallop. This proved to be a huge pack of *kairui*. As soon as the pack caught sight of them it stopped a moment in its wild course, made a noise similar to the grunting of pigs, and prepared for flight. With an awful clattering and gnashing of teeth, the troop rushed along in front of them.

There is equally no doubt that *huanganas* can be dangerous. Fountain had the profoundest respect for both species and had personally known three men cut to pieces, and was himself tree'd for two hours when, after shooting thirty-eight of the

herd, the remaining eleven moved off. Leonard Clark has recorded how he was tree'd by members of an immense herd of
huanganas leaping up at him, gouging the trunk with their tusks,
and attempting to dig out its roots. When the herd finally left
him, the entire river, from side to side, was a solid black mass of
huanganas—perhaps a thousand of them. That Clark was not
necessarily over-estimating the size of this herd is confirmed by
an experience of Up de Graff on the Napo, where he watched
a herd, estimated to be two thousand strong, swimming across
a river in a black mass at a point where it was a full 300yd broad:
when the leaders were climbing the far bank those in the rear
were still streaming down the bank on his side.

There is no doubt about the hunter's fear of peccaries. On one
occasion, when Manciet was shooting on the Madeira with his
Brazilian hunter, he noticed that the latter was looking anxious:

Something in the jungle was not normal: the silence, an oppressive
silence.

'Perhaps we'd better go back,' he said.

The words were hardly out of his mouth when we heard a
muffled sound, like distant thunder approaching.

'Quick—up a tree—it's *queixadas*!'

His face had gone white, and after a quick glance around him
he ran for a tree that was easy to climb.

Until that moment I had seen only one *queixada*, in Belem zoo:
it was an animal as big as a large pig that liked having his back
scratched. He would come up to the fence for this, and when anyone obliged he would close his little eyes and grunt with pleasure.
I had no intention of fleeing before a thing like that. I slipped a
bullet into the chamber of my .22 and waited—but not for long,
for soon the gaps in the trees about fifty yards away darkened
with a moving stream of brown.

I realised what an idiot I had been and leapt towards the first
tree I could find. I was astride a branch when they arrived, and
only then did I realise I had chosen my tree badly, for this one had
thorns as thick as my thumb all the way up its trunk, and I was
covered with blood.

As I was bleeding profusely, the creatures had picked up my
scent and were forming a circle round the tree, peering upwards

and clicking their jaws together like castanets. The ground was literally black with *queixadas*, hundreds of them.

Two hours later they were still there. Then I noticed that they were nosing about for truffles. With their enormous tusks they were rapidly digging up the earth round the foot of the tree— and all of a sudden I realised the danger. In the Amazon Basin the trees have horizontal roots, for the layer of soil where they find their nourishment is hardly ever more than eighteen inches deep.

Manciet then began shooting, with an experience similar to Fountain's, in as much as he was obliged to kill thirty-four before the remainder of the herd finally moved away.

4

Lesser Prey

Hunting deer and tapirs, and especially peccaries, must often involve a jaguar in hours of stalking and, in the end, failure to kill and eat. It may well be, then, that throughout the greater part of its range a jaguar's main source of food is, at weights of up to 120lb, the world's largest rodent: the capybara, sometimes known as the water-hog or water-haas or, in the Mato Grosso, as the *carpincho*. A capybara is a reincarnation on a small scale of prehistoric gargantua: a species of water guinea-pig the size of a small but very heavy, barrel-like, dark-brown sheep with short legs and cloven feet (which leave queer splayed footprints), a comic face, shrewd piggy eyes and, in Julian Duguid's words again, a snout carved by a novice out of a sloping tree-trunk. Capybaras are abundant on the borders of freshwater lakes and rivers, lying three or four, or exceptionally fifty or sixty together among the immense *Victoria regina* lilies and other aquatic plants during the day, frequently submerging for periods of up to eight or ten minutes; and stamping out well-trodden trails by night around the ponds and *bayous* in the marshes, where the jaguars catch them. Darwin found the Parana full of islands of muddy sand which, though inundated during periodic floods, held willows and other trees, bound together by a great variety of creepers to form a dense jungle retreat for both capybaras and jaguars. On the Parana, capybaras were the jaguars' main prey —as they were also, according to Azara, near rivers in the Paraguayan woods; and Darwin noted the coincidence that with the extermination of jaguars in the Maldonaldo region of the north Plata some years earlier, the capybaras had become very tame.

Darwin, amusingly enough, was much frightened by the sight of jaguars' tracks: but where capybaras are numerous man has little to fear from jaguars.

He who asked how the slow and clumsy giant anteater has been able to survive—'surrounded' by jaguars and pumas—was not well acquainted with the habits of an animal which is by no means as defenceless as its extraordinary appearance might suggest. This is not to say that jaguars do not attempt to prey upon anteaters, though according to Indians in the Mato Grosso they seldom do so; and Azara was wrong when he said that an anteater was no match for a jaguar, for it has immensely strong forefeet armed with huge claws, especially that of the middle toe. With these it opens up the rock-hard nests of termites—its main food—sucking up the insects with a tongue that can be extruded 24in from its narrow, toothless snout. Cherrie's Indian hunters told him that the liquids and juices from the eggs and nestlings of ground-nesting birds were also sucked up; but though he photographed one clinging to the trunk of a tree some 20ft above the ground, this had been hunted by a pack of hounds, and it is unlikely that giant anteaters deliberately climb trees in order to obtain eggs and nestlings. However, being the size of a small black bear, an anteater can strike formidably, and Indians in the Mato Grosso, the Guianas and Amazonia all agree that it can kill a jaguar by clasping it and forcing its claws into the latter's body, though it is usually killed itself in such an encounter.

If brought to bay, an anteater will rear up and, with swinging foreclaws, strike and rip up a man or hug him as it does a jaguar; or when being hunted by a dog, throw itself on its back and 'embrace' the dog when it springs at the throat, being powerful enough to crush the latter's ribs as if they were eggshells—as Cherrie expressed it. A 6ft specimen which George Gardner, the botanist, seized by the snout, rose up on its hind legs and clasped him round the waist with its forepaws, retaining its hold until hit repeatedly over the head with a stick. C. B. Brown was seized in the same way when he almost trod on a sleeping anteater; while an Indian hunting near Roraima, in British Guiana, and believed to have captured a young one, was found lying face downwards in the embrace of a dead female, one of whose claws had pierced his heart. Although the anteater had been stabbed in the back, its clasp was so vice-like that its forelegs had to be cut off before the Indian's body could be released.

Anteaters are perhaps offensive by nature, and Cherrie had the remarkable experience of being attacked by a *tamandua*, a very much smaller, arboreal anteater. He had paused to light his pipe when he heard a gentle movement in the bushes close beside him, and the next instant the queer snuffling characteristic of an angry *tamandua*. A second later one of these curious creatures burst through the bushes directly in front of him. It stopped, stared at him, and then to his surprise, started towards him with unmistakable signs of anger. When only a few feet distant it reared up on its hind legs and began to strike out with its forefeet. As the *tamandua* advanced, Cherrie parried its blows with his gun barrel and backed away. The creature followed, seemingly growing more furious with each ineffectual attempt to strike him; and finally, after backing away and escaping its blows a number of times, Cherrie's patience was exhausted and he shot it.

Giant anteaters have a wide range, and their numbers are probably much under-estimated since they are largely nocturnal, spending the day in the dense cover of thorny palm and cat-claw, though frequently on the move across open marsh where their pelage of coarse black hair illuminated by two white stripes renders them very conspicuous against the vivid green of the grass along the edges of the swamp. The fact that the swamp may be flooded to a depth of several inches does not inconvenience them in any way, since they can swim well and unexpectedly swiftly. Beebe, indeed, saw one making fair headway, though drifting rapidly downstream, across a river some 600yd broad, with only its elongated snout and head and the upper part of its bushy tail, waggling frantically with its exertions, protruding above the surface.

According to F. W. Miller, anteaters are great wanderers, and their characteristic trails lead across the grassy savannas from one thick brushy grove to another. In order that the huge claws, so vital to their livelihood, shall not be blunted they walk on the sides of the forefeet with the claws doubled back: but, when alarmed, lumber off in a clumsy, rocking, stiff-legged canter or gallop, with the immense bushy tail, held slightly above the horizontal and swaying loosely from side to side, streaming out behind like a banner. The anteater's tail, from 2 to 4ft in length, seems to serve several purposes. It may camouflage it from predators, for Fountain observed that a squatting anteater was completely hidden by its tail and resembled a tuft of dead grass. Since it also covers the head and shoulders of a sleeping anteater, it may provide warmth; while according to Wallace, it is also used as an umbrella: a habit of which Indians take advantage by rustling the leaves in imitation of rain and killing the animal with a blow on the head while it is sheltering beneath its tail.

So much for the jaguars' larger prey; but they are also active predators in the trees, climbing with surprising agility, running up branchless trunks as easily as a domestic cat runs up a clothes-post—as Fountain put it. Among their arboreal prey are two-toed and three-toed sloths: the latter smaller and distinguished by a black stripe down the centre of the back. So completely at odds are the various accounts of the behaviour of sloths that one despairs of discovering the truth about their habits in the wild state. However, in the vice-like grasp of their immense hooked claws, they resemble anteaters; and Schomburgk cites an instance in which only the combined strength of three Indians could relax a sloth's grip on the root-branches of a tree. But a sloth's claws are not offensive weapons, and for protection against such predators as jaguars, harpy eagles and large snakes, it must rely on various defensive measures, both cryptic and physical. Sloths, like howler monkeys, favour high, slender branches beyond the reach of jaguars, and pass much of their time sleeping in these inaccessible retreats, since they apparently

Page 51 With its great girth and stongly muscled forelegs a jaguar presents the appearance and strength of a tiger

Page 52 Young tapirs seek refuge in the water from the attacks of jaguars

require about twice as much sleep as other mammals; and much of their time hanging upside down below a branch, preferably at the thin end of one. To pluck a sloth from its vice-hold in such a position must present even a jaguar with a problem, particularly in view of the fact that its thick skin and two coats of fur are tough enough to turn an Indian's arrow. As additional protection, a sloth emits no detectable scent, has a keen sense of smell, and acute hearing. Moreover, it is virtually invisible—to the human eye—since its long, shaggy hair resembles withered grey grass, with a mossy tinge imparted by the algae that grow in the grooves of the hair. If any reader is disposed to doubt some of the tales that have been told about the animals of the South American jungle, let him take heed of the naturalist G. H. H. Tate who, when in Ecuador, confirmed by personal observation that a sloth's fur actually provides a breeding place for large numbers of a small moth, whose larvae, it is reasonable to presume, feed on the algae in the fur.

Stevenson tells us that when a sloth has reached the top of a tree it will remain there as long as a leaf is within reach, and even for some time afterwards, crying and howling, till hunger obliges it to search for food again. It then forms itself into a round lump and drops to the ground, as if devoid of life. This statement may be compared with Fountain's, that he had known one to drop 40ft on to hard ground, without injury, when attempting to escape from a jaguar. (A sloth has exceptionally broad flat ribs, and is almost as difficult to kill outright as a caiman.) While an anaconda might be evaded in this way, a jaguar obviously could not; and Lange was probably nearer the truth in his assertion that sloths usually fall accidentally when attempting to procure fruit hanging from branches that are too fragile to bear their weight. Actually, the three-toed sloths are reported to feed exclusively on the tender leaves of *cecropias*, purring contentedly as they swing backwards and forwards from their branches, holding a leaf by its stem and clipping round and round it until only a small disc remains about the stem. Fountain states that they also eat fruits, berries and gourds of various vines, all of which he found to have a strong acrid

D

flavour. In this instance, however, he may have been referring to the two-toed sloths which are less specialised in their feeding habits.

Hanging upside down, a sloth first extends one forepaw as far as possible along a branch and digs in its claws; then stretches the other to the same spot, and simultaneously drags along both hind feet, observed Schomburgk—adding that there might be as many as ten or twelve sloths feeding in one tree. In Fountain's experience, however, it was rare to find even two sloths in the same tree, though he agreed that one could always reckon on finding several more in other trees in the vicinity. That sloths should deliberately drop to the ground under any circumstances is manifestly improbable, for though the two-toed can walk with belly clear of the ground, the three-toed is virtually helpless, scarcely being able to do more than squirm around and advance ten yards in as many hours, according to Stevenson, howling most hideously and pitifully at each step—hence its Indian name *Ay* or *Ahi*. But a sloth is nothing if not persevering, physically and mentally. Lange observed that one brought in by Indians had succeeded by the following day in dragging itself across the village compound to a tree at its edge. And Konrad Guenther describes how he once saw a sloth attempting to climb from a palm into another tree. When it slung itself forward along a palm-leaf the leaf was pulled so far down by its weight that it was unable to reach the tree: 'Quietly it went back and embraced two palm-leaves, but as these were not rigid enough it made another attempt with three leaves, which did support its weight, and having reached the end of the three leaves, it was able to reach and grasp the nearest bough of the adjacent tree.'

Fountain roundly condemned all Stevenson's statements about the habits of sloths, observing that in his experience they were usually silent, though when angry or alarmed one would utter a sharp scream, and when captured almost weep; while, 'when pursuing the female he cries bitterly with a kind of blowing sob until he has captured her: the word "huff", strongly aspirated, gives a good imitation of the sound.' Under normal conditions, however, a sloth's whimper may be described as a feeble asthmatic whistle that penetrates only a few yards into the forest shades, and must be inaudible even to a sharp-eared jaguar, unless very close. Although Fountain also stated that a sloth displays a great dread of water, he was wrong in discrediting Henry Bates's assertion that he had watched one swimming across a river some 500yd in breadth, for Hamilton Rice, Schomburgk and Beebe all observed sloths swimming, and they have also been found on mid-stream islands. Beebe, indeed, watched them swimming rivers up to a mile wide on several occasions and estimated that one could cover a mile in 3 hours and 20 minutes—less than 10yd a minute. One that he marked was recovered twenty-eight days later, four miles within the jungle on the other side of a mile-wide river.

Fountain also disagreed with Bates's description of the sloth as the slowest creature on earth—a description otherwise universally concurred in, so far as I am aware, and embraced in the sloth's former scientific nomenclature *pregnica*, and also in the colloquially ironic *Perico ligero*, nimble Peter. But, says Fountain, this appreciation of the sloth, whether two-toed or three-toed, is erroneous and stems from the fact that, since it is mainly nocturnal, its true activity can only be studied at night—though under what circumstances can a sloth be watched at night? In his experience a sloth is nearly always asleep during the daytime:

Bringing all four feet quite close together on the same branch, and hanging back downwards, he buries the face in the hair of the chest and, wrapping the posterior part upwards over the nose, thus reposes, rolled into a rough ball. No doubt observers, seeing the animal spend the whole day in this position, and noticing, moreover, that while he is feeding his movements are slow and deliberate, have jumped to the conclusion that he is a slothful animal. But a sloth will travel from tree to tree through the forest so fast that not even the Indians can keep up with him for any distance. He invariably makes a bee-line for the best and easiest course, and never makes the mistake of passing to a part of the tree where he cannot without fail pass to another; and that in a forest so dense that it seems impossible that any animal can see the

direction it shall take. And he should be seen when he is alarmed
and desirous of escaping, or pursuing his lady-love. He only
hurries when there is occasion for haste, and even then his movements are so carefully timed, and have such an appearance of
deliberation, that it is not until you attempt to keep pace with him
that you discover how fast he is really going. His lady flees before
him from tree to tree, and travels at a great pace. When her lord
at length overtakes her, he clings to her as tenaciously as he does
to the bough of a tree; but thereafter they dwell amicably together
under the same foliage until her solitary cub is born.

Jaguars sometimes surprise monkeys by leaping upon them
from above, noted Fountain again, for despite their agility that
is the only way they can catch them. It was when he had reached
the upper waters of the Purus where, as we have seen, the land
was not so flat and less subject to flooding, and the forest less
impenetrable, that he began to observe the larger mammals,
which had been little in evidence in the densely forested and
flooded lower reaches. One morning when boating up the river
he observed a great commotion among a troop of black monkeys
with red faces. On altering course towards the bank to learn the
cause of this, he saw that a large jaguar was crouched on a
branch projecting some 20ft above the water, and that the
monkeys were leaping about him with wonderful agility, without however approaching near enough for the jaguar to seize
one of them. As the boat neared him, the jaguar climbed down
to a lower bough and, after looking at the men in a surprised
way for a minute or two, dropped into the water and swam to
an island, where he disappeared into a thicket.

There is, however, at least one species of monkey over which
the jaguar apparently exercises the same fearful fascination that
the tiger is reported to hold over the Indian *hanuman* monkey.
Descriptions of the procedure are almost identical in both cases.
W. L. Schurz describes, in *The Infinite Country*, a jaguar standing at the foot of a tall tree, gazing fixedly up into it, while from
the tip of the tree a *guariba* (the red howler monkey) is looking
down at the jaguar, while crying piteously and jumping from
side to side. The jaguar remains motionless: but the *guariba*,

still crying, descends lower and lower from branch to branch, and finally falls at the jaguar's feet. In normal circumstances the *guariba*, whose lower jaw is almost equal in size to the remainder of its head, is far from being defenceless. Up de Graff was attacked by one, after wounding it; and on his attempting to ward it off with his gun the *guariba* seized the barrel and closed the muzzle with its teeth.

One might be fanciful and declare that there is a curious affinity between jaguars and *guaribas*, for the awful serenades at sunrise and sunset of the adult males are not only so loud as to be comparable in volume to the jaguar's roar, but also include the latter's snarls and growls (and the grunting of peccaries):

> Then, without warning—[wrote Leo Miller on the Cauca in Colombia]—a sound so terrible rent the vast solitude that it seemed as if some demon of the wilds were taking a belated revenge for the few hours of quiet in which the earth had rejoiced.
>
> At first there was a series of low, gruff roars that would have done credit to the most savage of lions, and made the very air tremble. Then followed in quick succession a number of high-pitched, long-drawn wails or howls of tremulous quality that gradually died, ending with a few guttural barks. This uncanny performance lasted a number of minutes.
>
> The mists of night had lifted, revealing clumps of tall bamboo and the beginning of heavy forest. In the top of the very first trees sat a group of large monkeys, red, with golden backs.

'The first time I heard it,' said Up de Graff, 'it seemed that all the jaguars on the Amazon were engaged in a death-struggle.' Beebe was also reminded of the jaguar when he heard this roaring of the red baboons, as the *guaribas* are known in British Guiana:

> Then came an interruption, so sudden and unrelenting that it seemed to reach to the very heart of nature. A 'red baboon' raised his voice less than fifty yards away, and even the leaves seemed to tremble with the violence of the outburst of sound. A long, deep, rasping, vibrating roar, followed by a guttural inhalation hardly less powerful. After a dozen connected roars and inbreathings, the sound descended to a slow crescendo, almost died away and then broke with renewed force.

We saw two of the females giving voice with the leader, shrill falsettos which became audible only during the less inspiration.

We tried to think of a simile for the voice of this monkey and could only recur to that which always came to mind—the roar of the wind, ushering in a cyclone or terrific gale. And yet there was ever present to the ear the feeling of something living—as if mingled with the elemental roar was the howl of a male jaguar. No sound ever affected us quite as this; seeming always to presage some unnamed danger. While it lasted, the sense of peace which had been inspired by the calmness and silence of the jungle gave place to a hidden portent of evil.

The howling of the *guaribas* held a deep emotional appeal for Beebe, and on another occasion he wrote:

A low, soft moaning came through the forest. So low at first that it seemed but the hum of a beetle's wing echoing against the hollow shield of their ebony cases. It was deep, soothing, almost hypnotic. Then it gained in volume and depth until it became a roar, and from the heart of the bass there arose a terrible subdued trilling—a muffled raucous grating which touched some secret chord of long-past fear, when speech was yet unformed. The whole effect was most terrifying.

Now all with me were asleep, and alone I searched far out into the night and with mouth and ears absorbed every vibration of the wonderful chorus.

The red howler, one of five social and partly nocturnal species, is the largest of the South American monkeys, standing almost 3ft high and weighing up to 30lb, with a prehensile tail 2ft in length. Although the troops howl mainly at sunset and just before sunrise, any untoward incident will set them howling—a clap of thunder or sudden downpour, a passing aeroplane or even a flight of butterflies, or the approach of one of the large cats; and certainly their howling must proclaim the approximate whereabouts of a troop to every jaguar within a range of two or three miles. But its primary purpose is territorial. C. R. Carpenter, who watched a number of *guariba* 'clans' for a total of eight months on the island of Barro Colorado, has described how, when two clans meet, they conduct a vocal 'battle' which continues until one or other clan retreats; and F. M. Chapman listened to one outbreak that continued without intermission from 7am until 11am. Thus their howling advertises the locations of the various troops and the direction of their movements (on one occasion Schurz heard three troops bellowing at each other from different directions in the middle of the night), and regulates their territorial boundaries.

Leopold has described how, as the members of a troop look stiffly and gravely upon one another, the leader of the band, an old male with long silky beard, begins to warm up with a series of chesty roars. These gradually increase in frequency and volume until the sound is almost continuous. Then all the other members of the band join in, and the sound is multiplied manyfold. The bedlam may last for several minutes; but finally the old male gradually unwinds with a series of shorter roars, and his troop follow suit. Echo dies among the trees and is lost in the silence of the rain-forest.

'Squire' Waterton, hiding with characteristic bravado among the branches of a tall tree, listened with extreme astonishment to sounds that might have had their origins in the infernal regions, and noted the protuberance on the choir leader's inflated throat; for the adult *guariba's* deep jaws contain a remarkable extension of the cup-shaped hyoid apparatus, in the form of a hollow chamber in the throat, the size of a lemon, which serves as an amplifier. As he contracts the muscles of his barrel-like chest and stomach, air is forced under pressure across an opening at the top of the sound-box, producing the characteristic roar.

If you are curious to learn how this howl-box, this extension of the hyoid, evolved, then you must consult the Jivaro Indians through the medium of Up de Graff:

One day the *maquisapa* (the spider monkey) and the *coto* (the howler) met each other in the woods. The *coto* was showing the other how to break coconuts by pounding them together, but his long-legged cousin, when he tried to imitate him, caught his thumbs between the nuts and lopped them off. Determined to revenge their loss, when next he met his bearded friend he persuaded him by means of a sleight-of-hand that it was unnecessary to crack them at all, and that they tasted much better when swallowed whole. The credulous *coto* followed his advice, but the coconut stuck in his throat and left its mark on all his progeny to this day, while the children of the *maquisapa* must go for all time without their thumbs, although they still retain their toes.

5

Jaguars Fishing

Since the special habitat of jaguars is riverine jungle and swamp they must often come into conflict with caimans, and it is widely believed that the latter fear jaguars. Certainly, in the dry season when the rivers are low, both Indians and the *caboclo* half-breeds, are in the habit of imitating the jaguar's cry in order to scare caimans off the sandy *playas* into the water. Leonard Clark describes how an Indian who wishes to swim in the river may first call to the caimans in order to ascertain whether any are present. His loud grunting is apparently both audible and attractive to any caimans lying beneath the surface, and they rise in response to it.

Rolf Blomberg confirms the truth of this in an account of a night on the Apaya marshes of the San Miguel. A section of these marshes had previously been devastated by a forest fire—a rare phenomenon in the Amazonian jungle, one would suppose; and Blomberg found it difficult to describe the uncanny and fantastic appearance of La Apaya on that starry night as he and his companions glided slowly forward in their canoe over the dark water through the dead and mutilated marsh forest. Now and then a star seemed to detach itself from the sky and set out on a wandering flight—a firefly dancing through the darkness. The loud grating cries of toads mingled with the clear bell-like tones of tiny frogs:

> Villamizas sat in the bows of the canoe. He manoeuvred our slender craft, noiselessly and with great skill, through narrow channels and between fallen tree-trunks and debris. From time to time he imitated the mating cry of the caiman, uttering a loud *ao-ooo-*

oom! ao-ooo-oom! ao-ooo-oom! and striking himself hard on the chest, and often he received an answer from the depths of the marsh. Plenty of red eyes shone around us.

The terms caiman, alligator and crocodile have been employed indiscriminately by so many explorers that we had better put the record straight. There are, in fact, no alligators in Central or South America, but two species of crocodile and either five or seven species of caiman according to your preference. Since all are much alike in the field, it is helpful to remember that crocodiles are confined broadly to Ecuador, Colombia and Venezuela —though overlapping the caiman's range in the two latter states; and that though frequenting coastal creeks, they are restricted in rivers mainly to those reaches *above* the lowest falls or rapids. They are relatively small, with females averaging only 4 or 5ft in length, while 14ft is the maximum length for a male: whereas the largest caiman, the *jacarenassu* or *-asci*, reaches a length of 20 ft or possibly 25ft, though the largest among the thousands brought in to the Manaos tannery has not exceeded 16½ft.

Fountain, as it happens, never witnessed an encounter between jaguars and caimans, though he saw the latter pull deer underwater on several occasions and, in one instance, a large brown monkey lapping at the water's edge early in the morning. But both crocodiles and caimans are habitually killed and eaten by jaguars—especially the small *jacare-tinga* or *-tupi*, which reaches a length of only 6ft; and there have been many eye-witness accounts of conflicts between the two, with the smaller caimans being caught on the banks of ponds and *bayous*, and the larger while basking in the sun on the *playas* at some distance from water. Under such conditions, in Schomburgk's experience, a jaguar could always make a successful kill, provided that his talons did not become fixed in the caiman's belly plates. If this occurred, then the jaguar was liable to be dragged into the water and drowned. (A 13ft caiman weighs about 500lb.) All caiman kills found by F. W. Miller in the southern Mato Grosso, often at great distances from deep water, had been opened along the belly and bore teeth marks at the base of the head. Paul Le Cointe described to Schurz an encounter between a jaguar and a caiman he witnessed on the shores of the Trombetas. Le Cointe had emerged from the forest on to the edge of a low bluff that fell away to the flats along the river. Directly below him was a huge jaguar, intently watching a caiman that was waddling up the beach. Springing suddenly on to the caiman, the jaguar flipped it over with a paw and proceeded to feed on the soft underside of the neck. Finally, he turned his victim over again, whereupon the caiman returned to the water; but the blood from its neck quickly attracted a shoal of piranhas, which clung to the open wound as the unfortunate beast struggled to drag itself back up the beach.

According to Wallace, and also Herbert H. Smith, an American naturalist who travelled extensively on the Amazons in the 1870s, there have been many accounts of jaguars feeding on caimans, and particularly on their tails, while they were still alive. Wallace cites one instance of how, when a jaguar stopped eating and drew back a yard or two, its luckless victim would make a move towards the water, only for the jaguar to spring on it and resume eating its tail, while the caiman lay perfectly still. Prado witnessed a caiman being savaged in this manner by a large lynx (*sic*) which, with its paws on the caiman's tail, was tearing mouthfuls of the whitish flesh from its pale green belly while it was actually dragging itself down to the water. What is the peculiar nature of this macabre treatment that induces such a powerful beast to remain passive, and inhibits any attempt at retaliation?

A caiman's hold on life is, of course, so tenacious that a jaguar would have very great difficulty in actually killing one before beginning to feed on it. Yves Manciet gives an extraordinary illustration of this reptilian tenacity of life in an account of an incident on a tributary of the Araguaya. His party had killed a caiman, 5 or 6ft in length, by cutting its head clean off with a machete, and he and a companion were in the process of eating its cooked tail, when:

> I saw Zygmund's eyes widen and he let out a yell that woke the whole camp: 'Look, Yves, the alligator's getting away.'

It was quite true: the poor mutilated animal, who had been hacked up and apparently dead for a couple of hours, and whose head lay two hundred yards away, was walking slowly towards the river. It covered one yard—two—three, paused for a moment, started off again, and finally came to a halt several yards further on. None of us dared even breathe and our hair stood on end as we gazed incredulously at the walking corpse. The nightmarish sight had something terrifying about it, lit as it was only by the red glow of a dying fire, with a black sky above and pitch darkness all round, in the middle of almost unknown jungle.

The alligator seemed to have finished its walk: I went over and stirred it with the tip of my toe, but it did not move.

In every part of the world that they inhabit these antediluvian but extremely efficient saurians are being mercilessly exterminated. South America is no exception. According to Hakon Mielche, the State of Amazonas exported one million hides of caimans and crocodiles in a two-year period in the early 1940s. Whether or not we believe this monstrous figure, both Schurz and P. Matthiessen agree that the current conservation laws in Amazonia are totally inadequate and impossible to enforce. An interesting sidelight on this slaughter is given by Blomberg, who was told that the extermination of caimans on the island of Marajo at the mouth of the Amazon (an island as large as Belgium) had resulted in a most unwelcome increase in the numbers of snakes. However, there are still enormous numbers of caimans in such reaches of the Amazon as Manaos, where on the dark brown, oozing, slimy banks they are distinguishable from driftwood and logs only by their hazy-blue, metallic sheen.

At Iquitos, a thousand miles above Manaos, itself a thousand miles from the mouth of the stupendous Amazon, Leonard Clark's boat is tied up at a *playa* in the moonlight. A jaguar lumbers out of a strip of *canna* lilies. On seeing the boat it hesitates for a moment, then continues heavily and indifferently over to a fallen palm where it lies in the sand, reaching up with its claws and sharpening them on the trunk. Later it gets up, stretches and yawns, and walks across to a turtle—a *charapa*, weighing some 70lb, engaged in laying its eggs. Flipping the *charapa* out of its hole with its paws, the jaguar pounces on it, bites off the head and sets about digging the meat out of the shell.

Turtles (and their eggs) must form a considerable item in the menu of many jaguars. They are, or were, extraordinarily abundant in South American rivers, and have been reported lying as thickly as paving-stones over sand-bars two or three miles long and several hundred yards wide. The jaguars prey on the females when they plod out of the rivers to lay their leathery-skinned eggs in the sand. Patrolling the beaches and *playas*, the jaguars search for the turtles' broad trails, machine-like in the regularity with which the flippers' wash is kept equidistant by the structure of the carapace. Although the turtles weigh from 40 to 70lb, and in some cases as much as 300lb, they are invariably turned over on their backs; and Indians take advantage of the fact that a jaguar will turn over in one night many more turtles than he can eat.

> We cannot but admire [wrote von Humboldt] the suppleness of the tiger's paws, which empties the double armour of the *orraus*, as if the adhering parts of the muscle had been cut by means of a surgical instrument; and this he does by placing one paw on top of the turtle and skilfully biting out a round hole along the line of the junction between the back and front shields, through which he then scoops out the flesh with his paw and cleans out the shell without breaking it.

There is a long-standing and widespread Indian lore of a jaguar/fish association, and there is no doubt that jaguars are considerable fish-eaters, as one might expect them to be in a habitat so much of which is subject to perennial flooding. There are also records of ocelots and lynxes fishing. The fact that cats in general are proverbially supposed to dislike water has tended to obscure the truth that there have been many instances of domestic cats fishing, especially those living beside mill-pools; and not merely flicking a fish out with a paw, but actually diving for them. Some domestic cats have been seen to teach their kittens to fish; and when the Frenchman, F. Roulin, was on the upper Orinoco in 1824 an Indian told him that he had watched a jaguar catching fish at a small rapid and distributing them to her kittens: the latter, when they had eaten their fill, imitating her.

As long ago as 1750, Thomas Falkner had observed that the numerous jaguars on the south side of the river Plata preyed mainly on fish; and, according to Caspar Whitney, an island off Buenos Aires was at one time inhabited by several jaguars who subsisted mainly on fish. When Wallace was on the island of Mexiana in the mouth of the Amazon during the wet season, when much of the island was flooded, he described how a jaguar carried off at night large bundles of *pirarucu* (*Arapaima*) from a hut on the lakeside; and Up de Graff often saw jaguars on the Cusulina in Ecuador, swimming from bank to bank and splashing about in the shallows in pursuit of these gigantic freshwater fish, which may exceed 9ft in length and 400lb in weight, and are powerful enough to tear themselves free from a jaguar's talons and escape into deep water.

When fishing for moderately-sized fish, a jaguar takes up position on a log or branch projecting over the water and scoops them out with his paw. 'Jaguars often caught fish in our view,' noted Fountain. 'They took post on trees or roots lying half submerged, and beat the fish out of the water with their paws: it was always big fish they thus captured, and they never missed when they thus struck. We also saw them capture large water-fowl among the marginal herbage.' In Indian lore, however, a jaguar also catches fish by drooling saliva over a pool or, as Azara expressed it: 'The jaguar goes a little way out into the water, and there discharges some saliva, which attracts the fish, which the jaguar flips out on to the bank with his paw, but does not begin to eat them until he has thrown up a number.'

Those who have read my study of the Asian tiger may recall that the Mois of Viet-Nam claim that a small race of marsh tigers attract fish by dangling their tails in the water, flicking the fish out when they 'bite'. This sounds a very tall story but the belief that jaguars deliberately tap with their tails on the water in order to attract fish has always been so widespread in Brazil that the American ichthyologist, E. W. Gudger, considered it worth his while to investigate the evidence and to publish an exhaustive paper on his findings—to which I have been able to add one or two items.

Gudger established that hearsay evidence of jaguars fishing, from Indian sources, can be traced as far back as 1830 when a Swiss naturalist, J. R. Rengger, who lived in Paraguay for eight years, stated baldly that jaguars lured fish by tapping with their tails on the water and snatching them out with a paw when they rose. Some forty years later Stewart Clough, a missionary, noted in his journal written at Villa Bella near the junction of the Madeira with the Amazon: 'Here, too, the jaguar may often be seen engaged in piscatorial exercises, as he draws his tail backwards and forwards in the water till approached by his finny prey, when with lightning speed his sharp-clawed paw grasps the prize.'

Early in the nineteenth century La Cordière stated that jaguars in Brazil and Guiana habitually caught fish and crabs from rocks on the seashore; and in more recent years Theodor vom Koch-Grünberg, the ethnologist, 'was repeatedly assured, by both Indians and reputable white settlers, that the jaguar sits in the moonlight on the beach splashing the water with his long tail and throws the up-coming fish out on to the dry land with one stroke of his broad paw'.

The question is: why should fish rise when a jaguar taps with his tail or draws it through the water? The obvious answer is because their curiosity is aroused by the disturbance, or vibrations, in the water and by the sight of the jaguar's tail. That would be a sufficient answer, but it is not the full answer, as Wallace was the first to indicate more than a hundred and twenty years ago when he recorded that, according to the Indians, when a fishing jaguar lashes his tail in the river he imitates falling fruit. Subsequently, Herbert Smith obtained from Indians on the Tapajos and other northern tributaries of the Amazon a more detailed account of this jaguar-fish-fruit association: 'The jaguar, they say, comes at night and crouches on a log or branch over the water; he raps the surface with his tail gently, and the *tambakis*, or other fruit-eating fish come to the sound, when he knocks them out with his paw.'

According to A. C. de Magalhaes, a Brazilian ichthyologist, these *tambaquy* fish feed on the fruits of various trees and bushes, which grow along the banks of the streams and ripen during the season of high water, when they are eaten by birds. The berries that fall into the stream cause a characteristic sound and disturbance in the water, attracting the *tambaquys*, which swarm around the berries and swallow them. The Indians, who take advantage of this habit to catch these fish, assert that they learned to do so by watching jaguars. Taking up its position on a leaning trunk at the edge of the water or in the shade of an *igapo* tree on the bank, a jaguar taps the water with the tip of its tail, to simulate the noise of falling fruit. When the fish rush towards the sound, the jaguar scoops them out or dives in after them.

In this respect it is interesting to note that the Djukas of Surinam assert that the *cumaru* fish shoal under a *walaba* tree when its seed-pods are ripening, surfacing for the seeds whenever a pod explodes with a loud pop. This implies that the fish actually hear the explosion of a pod; and according to the Djukas, when the *walabas* are not seeding the *cumaru* will still respond to the sound of hand-clapping and rise, to be harpooned or scooped out of the water. That jaguars select fruit trees overhanging the water from which to capture frugivorous fishes (without necessarily employing their tails) is also attested by Indians in the Mato Grosso.

So much for hearsay evidence from Indian tribes scattered over some three million miles of Brazil and Paraguay: but we have also some evidence from Europeans. In his *Explorations of of the Valley of the Amazon*, Lieut W. L. Herndon included many sound natural history notes. During the course of his three-year descent of the Amazon he met a French engineer, A. M. de Lincourt, who had been exploring the cataracts on the Tapajos (subsequently visited by Herbert Smith). From Lincourt's journal, Herndon extracted the following note on the Frenchman's experiences at the foot of the fifth cataract where, since his

Indian crew were exhausted, he kept the night watch because of the presence of large numbers of jaguars and other cats:

> Walking along the beach to prevent sleep, I witnessed a singular spectacle but (as I was informed by the inhabitants) one of frequent occurrence. An enormous tiger was extended full length upon a rock, level with the water, about forty paces from me. From time to time he struck the water with his tail, and at the same moment he raised one of his forepaws and seized a fish, often of enormous size. These last, deceived by the noise, and taking it for the fall of forest fruits (of which they are very fond), unsuspectingly approach and fall into the claws of the traitor. I did not interrupt him, and when he was satisfied he went off.

And finally there is the direct testimony of Le Cointe that he had seen jaguars imitate the effects of fruit falling into the water by giving the surface a light blow with the tail and, when inquisitive fish came up for the supposed fruit, strike a lightning blow with a paw and haul them ashore.

While no one has yet photographed jaguars 'angling', the above evidence that they do so must be considered reasonably conclusive; and circumstantial evidence that angling may not be restricted only to jaguars among the cats comes unexpectedly from what may be described as suburbia, in an account given to Gudger by a householder in North Carolina of events at his backyard fish-pool, which was heavily stocked with goldfish. His neighbours' cats and dogs came to drink at this pool, and sometimes one of the cats, when drinking, would sit on a stone projection built into the rim of the pool above the water. In due course the goldfish began to disappear; and his grandchild told him that she had seen a large grey tomcat, which belonged to a neighbour, catching the fish. He found this difficult to believe until he himself saw the tom in the act. Apparently the latter had observed that the fish would surface when the water was disturbed, and had learned to sit on the rock projection with its tail in the water and wriggle it in order to attract the fish, snatching them out when they surfaced.

We cannot conclude this account of jaguars fishing without asking whether they are ever attacked by those atrociously

E

bloodthirsty little fish, the piranhas or *perais*, or *caribes*, which are reported to be capable of biting through a heavy fish-hook with a single stroke of their saw-edged teeth? Tapirs sometimes bear the scars of their fearful teeth, and caimans with toes missing are often shot. Piranhas are relatively small bass-like fish (averaging only 8in in length and 1lb in weight, though individuals 2ft long and weighing 8 to 10lb have been recorded), and are restricted mainly to slow-moving waters, rarely frequenting the white water of rapids. There has been a tendency to pooh-pooh both their savagery and potential danger. Peter Fleming, for example, recounted how he and his companions waded all day among shoals of piranhas in the Tapirate river without being attacked; and Hendrik de Leeuw was sceptical of the tales about their savagery until he witnessed with his own eyes a peccary attacked by a shoal of them and completely stripped of its flesh in two minutes. But Indian tribes—the Caragas on the Araguaya for one—are extremely cautious in waters infested by the 'little doves', as they are ironically known; and to ascertain whether any shoals are present, clap cupped hands below the water, producing a peculiar sound, or vibration, which invariably attracts them. Normally piranhas attack only when attracted by the sight or scent or some other property of blood, and the merest scratch suffices. In this respect, Prado describes the perhaps significant tragedy of a girl in a *scarlet* bathing costume who was killed (merciful word) by piranhas after diving from a boat into the Canuma river in the serras south of the Amazon; and there is some evidence that they are not attracted by the black skin of a Negro, though they are by the pale soles of his feet.

George Cherrie, when fishing for piranhas from the limb of a tree projecting over the water, overbalanced, and as he fell tore a long gash in his arm. Although he rolled about and splashed violently with arms and legs, he was severely bitten before he could swim the few yards to the shore, and carried the scars for the rest of his life. But piranhas will also attack when there is no blood in the water. General Candido Rondon, first chief of Brazil's Indian Protection Service, had a toe bitten off by a piranha when he was bathing, and many Indians have lost fingers when dipping their paddles too low in the water; while Sacha Siemel saw a white man, a Scandinavian, disembowelled when swimming across the Taquari river in Brazil. On the Venezuelan *llanos*, those vast, perenially flooded grasslands broken by wave-like masses of forest, piranhas are particularly feared, and Don Ramon Paez describes how a *vaquero* was attacked when swimming a drove of horses across the Portuguesa.

'Never in all my life have I seen such a display of unbridled viciousness'—wrote Wolfgang Cordan of attacks by piranhas on the body of a tapir he had shot in a river: 'Voracious, teeth-filled jaws, all snapping and tearing at the carcass, and even at one another.' The tapir's body had sunk some 6ft to a bottom of white sand, and while he and his companion were looking down at it a terrific commotion began to take place round the dead animal. Then, in no time at all, their dugout was in the centre of madly churning water, lashed to foam by the frenzied gyrations of thousands of piranhas. The creek seemed to be alive with the bloodthirsty creatures, all gone stark raving mad with the smell and taste of blood, and even leaping out of the water and falling into the boat. When parts of the tapir's dismembered body floated to the surface they instantly became the focal points for renewed battles among the piranhas.

6

The Anaconda

The haunts of the anaconda in tropical South America east of the Andes (and also in Trinidad) are swamps and rivers, especially swamps because these do not dry out during the rainless season as do many of the smaller streams. Teeming with deer, peccaries, tapirs, capybaras and those giant guinea-pigs, the *pacas* or *labas*, together with caiman, turtles, large fish and waterfowl, these haunts are also, as we have seen, those of jaguars; and no doubt encounters between giant snake and great cat are not rare. According to Roosevelt, a jaguar will pounce on and kill an anaconda; and Fountain's verdict was: 'I know that the jaguar is very fond of snake's flesh, and frequently attacks anacondas, and the boa also. I think fights sometimes take place, for I found the carcass of a jaguar, which showed every appearance of having been killed by a constricting snake, which afterwards seemed to have made an attempt to swallow it, and failed on account of its great size.'

Yuca-Mammam (Mother, or Great One, of the Waters), *sucuruju* or *sucuriju*, *kamudi*, *joboa*, *water boa*—but *not* boa-constrictor—the anaconda is the largest of several species of boa, reaching lengths that certainly exceed 40ft: whereas the true boa-constrictor is a considerably smaller snake, not known to exceed 18 or 19ft in length, with a thin neck and a tail that narrows to a point. Its girth, however, can be immense; and Fountain claimed to have shot a 17ft specimen which, though its stomach was empty, had a circumference of 52in. Although both anacondas and boa-constrictors occur in the same localities over much of tropical South America, the latter are mainly arboreal: whereas anacondas are mainly aquatic and seldom found far from permanent water, in which they pass much of their lives, either motionless with only nostrils and eyes (protected by transparent watertight shields) exposed, or undulating along the bottom of shallow creeks. They can remain submerged for upwards of ten minutes; and the Suke Napis of the Putamayo are reported to kill them by paddling slowly to and fro, scanning the bottom of a clear shallow stream until they spot one lying on the bottom, when it is tapped lightly on the head with the butt end of a spear and lanced as it surfaces.

Opinions differ as to the speed at which anacondas swim, though in Blomberg's experience they swim so fast that it is impossible to capture them in deep water; but they do not generally hunt in water, though the smaller ones catch small fish and frogs, and Beebe removed twenty-seven fish, including sharp-spined, armoured cat-fish, from the stomachs of three large specimens. When not in the water an anaconda is likely to be coiled like an anchor rope around a thick branch projecting over a river or creek, with a few feet of 'neck' and that extraordinarily flat head swaying over the water, as it contemplates the traveller's canoe with its inordinately large and inexpressive eyes; or stretched out torpid along a log or on a sand-bar, especially after a spell of cool or rainy weather, for like most snakes anacondas are great sun lovers. But on those infrequent occasions when an anaconda is hungry it becomes restless and voracious and, with its tail looped securely round a branch, is prepared to drop on any prey passing beneath, whether this be a caiman or a canoe, a peccary or a jaguar, or sometimes a man: any error in estimating the size of the prey can be rectified after the attack has been made. (One wonders how anacondas prey on wild dogs, as according to Fountain they often do.)

An anaconda may also attempt to track a small mammal to its hole, 'scenting' the trail by touch with its tongue, which stimulates a sense organ in the roof of the mouth. Its world is predominantly one of 'smell', and its flickering tongue is continually testing the air. It has no external ears and lacks sensitivity to airborne sounds, though it is probably aware of ground vibrations.

Since an anaconda has no vocal apparatus and can only fill its lungs and hiss for half a minute or so at a time (a deep hoarse hiss, like the sound of steam escaping from a radiator, that can be distinctly heard at a distance of 100ft), Fawcett would appear to have been mistaken in attributing certain melancholy nocturnal wails to this source. Only an expert naturalist can determine the innumerable strange and often terrifying sounds to be heard at night in the South American jungle. Sadly, South America has been ill-served in this respect. Had there been a few more of William Beebe's calibre what might we not have known? It was in Venezuela that Beebe noted in his journal:

> We hear at our very feet the muffled choking sigh which has come to us every night since we entered the mangrove swamp. Now the mystery solves itself as a large anaconda, nine or ten feet long, slowly winds out from a hole in the bank beneath the surface of the water and slips into the depths of the muddy current. Then the tide laps a little lower, and a big bubble of air, caught in the entrance of the serpent's lair, frees itself with a sudden gasping sob. When the tide is rising or falling over these large openings in the mud the air escapes from time to time with the terrifying sound which has so long puzzled us.

Fountain gave a singularly accurate, though loosely-written, description of the technique employed by an anconda in engorging its prey, which I have paraphrased:

> I have noticed that when an anaconda hangs head downwards it always has more than one coil of the tail wrapped around the bough from which it is suspended. When it seizes prey in this position, which it often does as the victim passes under the tree, if the latter is of large size the snake always comes to the ground to eat it. The act of swallowing is a slow process, as is the previous one of killing the victim. Fold after fold of the horrid body is wrapped round the struggling victim and the pressure slowly applied, the serpent frequently relaxing its pressure and permitting the victim partially to revive. It never bites its prey: the teeth being singularly small, and curved backwards towards the throat, being evidently intended simply to prevent the food slipping back from the gullet during the process of swallowing, as it stretches

and grips, stretches and grips again slowly and laboriously, with each further engulfment of the victim: the two halves of the lower jaw working independently. The more its prey struggles to pull away the deeper the snake's teeth sink into its body. A great deal of saliva runs from the snake's mouth during this process, but it does not deliberately shed it over the prey for the purpose of lubricating it. The prey is killed by suffocation, the result of intense pressure; but the bones are not broken.

Hours may pass while a giant snake eats one of its prodigious meals, for a great deal of its time is spent in resting and in pausing to breathe through the heavily reinforced glottis, which is periodically forced forward between the prey and the tightly stretched floor of the mouth. But the only qualification with which Fountain's observations might be improved, after the lapse of more than eighty years, is that, according to some observers, saliva flows only after a frightened snake has vomited up its prey. One can also enlarge, with P. R. Cutright's assistance, on the cause of death:

> After seizing its prey in vice-like jaws, the serpent coils its body about its opponent and squeezes. The muscular pressure is sufficient to keep the chest from expanding and thus halt the ability to breathe. Death is to be attributed to the stoppage of the heart. It would appear that the snake is very sensitive to the heartbeat of its victim and following each systolic action the snake, in perfect rhythm, increases the pressure. This deprives not only the lungs of the needed space for action, but the heart as well. As a result the heart soon stops its action, death following at once.

From this analysis it follows that there is no necessity for an anaconda to break the bones of its victim, as it is popularly supposed to do, though this can occur. But despite the fact that the elastic texture of the skin and ligaments of both upper and lower jaws enables an anaconda to engulf a victim several times its own diameter, the latter may, if it is of an awkward shape, be squeezed into a form that can be more conveniently swallowed. However, certain kinds of prey possess appendages that cannot be moulded into shape—a deer's antlers, for example. A Dutch friend of Charles Waterton killed a 22ft anaconda which had a pair of stag's horns protruding from its jaws; and Up de Graff describes in *Head Hunters of the Amazon* how:

> While out hunting on the trail I was attracted by a peculiar move-ment among the shorter growth. Suddenly, ten feet above the ground, there came into view a long thin neck surmounted by a head with a pair of horns (or tusks perhaps) which swayed from side to side as if in search of prey. The horns, however, instead of rising from the crown of the head, projected sideways. 'If this is its neck,' I thought, 'what will its body be like?' And then there flashed through my mind a possible solution. 'The *Diplodocus* at last!'
>
> As I watched for the beast to expose its body its neck lurched forward and it hooked its horns among the tangled vines which clung to the tree. The neck withdrew, leaving what I had taken to be the animal's head suspended from the vines, the putrid skin sticking to the skull from which there still hung two or three vertebrae. Then it was I recognized the phenomenon which I had come across once or twice before, the head of a deer hanging from a tree. The anaconda—for such it was—after ridding itself of that portion of its prey which it could not swallow, withdrew slowly to find a spot where it could sleep off its meal in peace.
>
> Apparently these reptiles cannot negotiate the head of a spike-horn deer; so they swallow the body and wait until they can break off the half-rotten head from the partly digested trunk. That they must wait a considerable length of time before they can accomplish this feat is certain, for the head of which I saw that anaconda rid itself was already in an advanced state of decomposition. After-wards I learned from the Indians that what I had seen is of common occurrence in the forest.

Having finally engorged its victim, there remains for the ana-conda the problem of digesting this bulky object with which its stomach is enormously distended. In this it is assisted by gastric juices powerful enough, it is reported, to dissolve the bones and horny hide of a caiman, though it sometimes dis-gorges balls of horn and hair from small deer. It is usually said that even a large anaconda (measuring upwards of 26ft, with a coil thickness of 12in, and weighing between 300 and 400lb) has to strain when swallowing a 100lb pig, and that a 150lb prey would be the largest with which any anaconda could cope; but considering the various animals known to have been swallowed by anacondas, this would appear to underestimate their capacity. Manciet, for example, was guided to a remote place near a small river where, according to an old *caboclo*, one of his cows (which could hardly have weighed less than 250lb, however emaciated) had been eaten by an anaconda some months earlier, and which he feared would take another one—anacondas being territorially conservative; and there: 'Coiled round a thick branch, his head swaying a couple of yards below, was the monster. His head looked disproportionately small, for it was not more than six inches long, whilst the serried coils round the branch appeared enormous and endless.'

There is also the statement by Paez, whose father owned many ranches on the Venezuelan *llanos*, that anacondas frequently attacked not only colts and calves but also the herd bulls. This was confirmed by Arthur Friel, who observed that these anacondas of the *llanos* invariably struck at a bull's nose when it was drinking, and were able to retain their hold, though lying on the soft mud of a lagoon lacking any rock or stump around which they could coil their tails. On occasions a bull might cut a snake in two with its hooves and make off with half of it still hanging from its nose.

And why should one doubt George Gardner's testimony in *Travels in Brazil* that:

In the marshes of this valley, near Arrayas, the boa constrictor [anaconda] is often met with of considerable size; particularly by the wooded margins of lakes, marshes and streams. Sometimes they attain the enormous length of forty feet. Some weeks before our arrival at Safe, the favourite riding-horse of Senor Lagorina, which had been put out to pasture not far from the house, could not be found. Shortly after this, one of his *vaqueiros*, in going through the wood by the side of a small river, saw an enormous boa suspended in the fork of a small tree which hung over the water; it was dead, but had evidently been floated down alive by a recent flood, and being in an inert state it had not been able to extricate itself from the fork before the waters fell. It was dragged out to the open country by two horses, and was found to measure thirty-seven feet in length; on opening it the bones of a horse in a somewhat broken condition, and the flesh in a half-digested state, were found within it, the bones of the head being uninjured; from these circumstances we concluded that the boa had devoured the horse entire.

No doubt an anaconda would find such an active and powerful beast as a jaguar a difficult prey to tackle, and would not attempt to do so unless itself attacked, though it would have the advantage if near water. However that may be, there is no doubting the frequency of encounters between anacondas and the formidable caimans; and J. H. Moore refers to a 'well-authenticated' account of an anaconda and a caiman which were locked in almost motionless combat for more than two weeks before the snake ultimately succeeded in killing the caiman. Although one may doubt this, the German naturalist and archaeologist, Friedrich Morton, did in fact photograph an encounter that lasted from one afternoon until the next in a sandy hollow of the Rio Nino at the edge of a Guatemalan jungle. He describes how he was watching some crocodiles basking on the river sand when a 20ft anaconda swung down from the lianas to stretch itself in the sun. Suddenly there was a spurt of sand, and the anaconda had wrapped three tight coils around the hindquarters of one of the crocodiles. Thereafter the struggle proceeded purposively, though with frequent intervals of rest, while the crocodile strove to reach the water, threshing its tail violently in the shallows and endeavouring to reach the anaconda with its jaws. By nightfall, the protagonists had disappeared in the opaque waters. The next morning, however, Morton was amazed to find them still lying in the shallows, and was able to photograph them. During the night the anaconda had succeeded in wrapping a fourth coil around the crocodile; and although the latter whipped itself about for several hours on this second day, hurling itself into the water and swimming, crawling back up the beach again and rolling in the sand, this coil was gradually constricted. Late in the afternoon the crocodile died, and the anaconda, itself severely hurt, slowly uncoiled, to lie motionless for a long period.

In some instances an anaconda's great length enables it to hold a caiman below water until it drowns, while keeping its own head above water. Guppy photographed one killing an 8ft crocodile in this way. When shot, it proved to be 17¼ft in length, with a diameter of 9in at the middle and 6in behind the head. It had been severly gashed by the crocodile's teeth, while the latter's head was loose, as if its spine had been snapped, though there were no indications of its body having been crushed.

However, the anaconda is not always the victor, for Fountain describes how he once saw a caiman seize an anaconda, possibly 16 or 18ft in length, which was lurking on the brink of the river Coroa. In spite of furious lashings and writhings it was dragged underwater, and doubtless killed. With a victim of this size a caiman would not begin its meal immediately, but would hide the carcass in a hole, or under a bank, and wait for it to decompose. Fountain suggests that many of those dead anacondas that are to be seen floating in Brazilian rivers have been killed by caimans.

Anacondas in zoos thrive on three or four meals a year, since they are estimated to consume in one meal four hundred times their daily energy requirements, and they are known to be able to survive for two and a half years without food. In the wild state, however, they no doubt feed much more often than this, and Beebe mentions a 10ft female which took a chicken from a hen-house in Guiana on seven successive nights. (According to Bates, anacondas were often to be found curled up in farmyards in some parts of Amazonia). For four or five days after a gorge an anaconda is virtually incapacitated, though possibly its reluctance to move may be in order to avoid internal injury. In this state it must prove easy prey for a jaguar—and sometimes for peccaries, for H. S. Dickey witnessed a herd of some thirty peccaries kill a 'great snake' with ease, cutting it to shreds with their sharp hooves. A full-fed snake will continue to be inactive and relatively inoffensive, or perhaps semi-torpid, for a considerable period. Up de Graff, who saw only four anacondas during his seven years in Amazonia, encountered one in this semi-torpid condition:

Having sighted the great reptile coiled up on a fallen tree which lay half in the water, half on the bank, we paddled quietly up to within a yard or two for closer inspection. It lay in a pyramid of coils, apparently sleeping. Surprised that it did not move, we splashed water on it to wake it up; there being no result, I started to prod it with my paddle, and still meeting with no success, I lifted my paddle and brought it down on the snake's side with a resounding whack that actually broke the blade. It squirmed a little, but soon lay still again. Determined to get a closer view, I climbed out on to the log and kicked the fat black coils. It showed some signs of animation, so I finally got back into the canoe and continued to prod it. Finally, it awoke, slipped into the water while still half rolled up, and swam leisurely away on the surface, giving us a good chance to judge its length. Comparison with the twenty-four foot canoe showed it to be some thirty feet long.

Instances of anacondas attacking men are rare, and neither they nor boas 'constrict' when attacked, but strike and attempt to bite. Schomburgk, however, recorded an encounter with an 18ft anaconda (the largest he ever saw) which was lying inactive in a swamp emitting a very offensive smell. When wounded it rushed towards him, obliging Schomburgk to retreat.

In fact no known snake can overtake a running man, since the swiftest can only cover from 200 to 250yd a minute, while the large snakes are very much slower. Certainly, neither anacondas nor boas are much feared in general. Matthiessen conducted an enquiry among the Indians and other inhabitants of Amazonia as to what animals, whether mammal or reptile, they considered the most dangerous. Their response was headed by two snakes —first the bushmaster, and second the fer-de-lance. Schurz confirmed this finding, with the addition of the rattler. Amazonians differentiate between three kinds of bushmasters: the *surucura*, the *pico de jaca*, and the *apaca fogo*. The latter is known as the 'fire-extinguisher' because of its habit of coiling up on the ashes of smouldering fires, and is feared so much by forest men that they never keep their fires alight at night. The most remarkably unpleasant trait of the bushmaster is that if one of a pair is killed or molested, its mate will attack immediately and, despite what has been said above, moves with extraordinary speed. Victor Norwood was twice trailed in this way after killing one of a pair, and Matthiessen observed how, before striking, the bushmaster drives the horny hook at the base of its tail into the ground in order to achieve rigidity and balance. But poisonous snakes are comparatively rarely encountered by the traveller in South America. Schurz saw only two (at one time) during his 25,000 miles of exploration. It is the *caboclo*, working with his machete in tall grass or light undergrowth, who suffers most severely, particularly in the *cerrado* (the bad-lands) of the Mato Grosso and the *coatinga* country of north-eastern Brazil.

There are, however, authentic records of attacks on man by anacondas, some recent. Schurz was a witness to one in which an anaconda, with its tail looped around a branch, had coiled itself about a man. When killed and stretched it measured $27\frac{3}{4}$ft, with coils 14in in diameter. When on the Orinoco, Arthur Friel was told of three instances of attacks by anacondas. In one an anaconda, hanging from a branch, coiled itself around a canoe and a man sleeping in the moonlight on top of a load of *balata* (rolls of rubber), but was killed with machetes by other members of the crew who were sleeping in hammocks on shore. In another, a man was struck in the hand when he dipped it into the water while cleaning a duck at the edge of a rock, but he was able to hold to the rock with his other hand until the anaconda had been killed by his companions. In a third instance a man washing clothes at the edge of a stream was also seized by the hands and pulled into the water. He was not seen again.

Kurt Severin refers to an 'authenticated' attack in which a man watering cattle in a tributary of the Napo was 'coiled' round the legs and pulled into the water and drowned; and Blomberg to two cases—in one of which a man was seized when swimming in the Napo, while in the other a thirteen-year-old boy was pulled under when swimming at the mouth of the Yasuni (another tributary of the Napo). In this instance the anaconda was found thirty hours later lying half in and half out of the water, having disgorged the boy. It is possible that snakes have their likes and dislikes where food is concerned, but there is no questioning a large snake's ability to engorge a boy, because there is a bona fide record of a fourteen-year-old Malayan boy being cut out of the stomach of a 17ft reticulate python.

A hungry anaconda will be attracted in the first instance to any moving object, as was the case with one which was seen to swim from the nearby shore when a passenger on a ferry (crossing a lagoon in Trinidad) dived overboard for a bathe, and seized the man by his single undergarment, tearing it off while its owner escaped. Normally, however, an anaconda is as anxious to avoid man as most other wild animals. Duguid encountered a 15ft anaconda moving through marsh grass in the Mato Grosso with its spade-shaped head an inch or two above the ground, and had the temerity to seize it by the back of the neck: 'whereupon its small dark eyes went black and its tail lashed like a whip'. However, when he dropped it, it made off immediately. Bates also came 'face to face' with an anaconda advancing down a slope, making the dry twigs crack and fly with a sound of rushing wind. On becoming aware of him, it turned suddenly and, with Bates following, accelerated: 'Its rapidly moving and shining body looked like a stream of brown liquid flowing over the thick bed of fallen leaves, rather than a serpent with a skin of varied colours.'

To those who are not repelled by snakes, an anaconda is a beautiful creature. To the Cauclos Indians on the river Bobonaza (a tributary of the Maranon) the rainbow is a gigantic anaconda arching the world, or the shadow of an anaconda. Stevenson wrote in his journal of his great surprise and delight when, on entering the mouth of the Quininindi (a tributary of the Esmeraldas), he encountered two anacondas basking on a sandbank, very near to the edge of the water:

> We passed them at a distance of about twenty feet. One appeared to be at least twenty-five feet long, the other about half that length. They were both of them in the most beautiful postures that can be imagined, their heads raised, and their bodies forming festoons or arches; those formed by the greater one were six, the largest in the centre being about two feet high; the smaller formed only five arches, and these were much lower than the other. Their colours were a most brilliant yellow, a deep green, and stripes along the

back of a dark brown hue. The tremulous motion of these animals, occasioned probably by the posture in which they had placed themselves, gave to their colours a most imposing effect; the brilliancy was heightened too by the rays of the sun darting full upon them; I felt as if I were under a charm, and I sat gazing on them in a transport of delight for more than half an hour.

These two were presumably in courtship. Normally the ana-conda apparently leads a solitary existence: but there have been occasional reports of numbers together. Shortly before Blom-berg arrived at the junction of the Caucaye and the Putamayo, the local hunters told him they had found eleven in a tangle on the beach, of which the largest measured about 20ft; and Lange, when traversing a vast forest swamp, came upon a pond-like hole filled with a writhing mass of semi-torpid, blue-grey ana-condas varying from 6 to 20ft in length. Some lay below the surface of the lukewarm ooze, others on the bodies of these.

Anacondas have been reported as giving birth to from twenty-eight to forty-two young, and possibly as many as seventy-two, averaging from 2 to 3ft in length. Schomburgk saw large num-bers of young ones, 5 or 6ft long, in trees projecting over a creek of the Barina; and Harold Noice describes how his attention was attracted by a vicious hiss, loud and terrifying. On turning, he saw on the other side of the log, not 10ft distant, a huge anaconda coiled in a damp shallow pit, with all about it a seething mass of at least fifty young ones, 3ft long and about 1in in diameter. Raising its head high, the anaconda reared its neck back and bared long curved teeth. Its dark green coils, patterned symetri-cally with black spots and circles, were beautiful yet terrible.

7

'Sucuriju Gigante'

Gigantic reptiles, together with the activities of Colonel P. H. Fawcett, are the two subjects one would tactfully avoid mentioning at any average gathering of authorities on the fauna and exploration of the South American jungle. For zoologists, though now conditioned by the shocks to their orderly files of such miraculous resurrections as the 'long-extinct' coelacanth, are still reluctant to admit the possibility of any new discovery smacking of the incredible, or even more repugnant, of the supernatural. Similarly, there has been a natural revulsionary reaction among explorers to the varied and numerous sensational rumours associated with the disappearance of Colonel Fawcett, though in fact scores of unremembered 'Fawcetts' and 'Maufrais' of many nationalities have also disappeared into the South American jungle in just as mysterious, if unpublicized, circumstances. Scientists like to present the image of being honest men, who will not accept any fact or fiction that they cannot prove for themselves. But, logically, it is both unscientific and dishonest to refute the incredible if you yourself are not in a position to do so because you were not a personal witness of it. Judgement on the incredible should only be accepted or refuted if the weight of evidence for or against is overwhelming. If such evidence is lacking then judgement should be suspended. When Algot Lange, after killing and measuring a gigantic anaconda, lamented that his friends in the USA would not believe his tale, his Indian companion asked him why *he* should believe in Lange's statement that in his country thirty-five or forty houses were built one on top of the other.

Page 88 The giant anteater, capable of killing a jaguar

In considering the case for or against the likelihood of gigantic serpents still existing, Professor Arnold Van Gennep has made a most significant point to the effect that: the memory of an historical fact does not continue among communities *which do not use a written language* for more than five or six generations, that is to say for a hundred and fifty years on the average, and two hundred years at most. If he is correct, then it follows that since none of the Indian tribes in the South American jungles has a written language, all traditions or legends of gigantic serpents or fabulous creatures are based on material dated long after the arrival of the first Europeans. Indeed, since some of these legends are still current, they could stem from a no more distant past than the early nineteenth century. This is a factor always to be borne in mind when examining the 'incredible', as is a second factor—that only those who are permanent inhabitants of the jungle ordinarily encounter many snakes. The explorer in transit is unlikely to see many snakes, large or small, harmless or venomous, for obvious reasons; and, as Matthiessen has pointed out, it is possible to walk (with clumsy tread and noisy companions) for days at a time through the jungle and not *see* a single snake—or jaguar for that matter. Moreover, the largest anacondas, 30ft or more in length, usually inhabit ponds or swamps away from the rivers that are man's only highway through hundreds of thousands of square miles of jungle.

Since the abrupt and contemptuous dismissal of all reports of gigantic snakes and rumours of 'unknown' reptiles has always irked me, I have taken this opportunity of going over once again the available material on the size of anacondas. In considering records or rumours of very large snakes, it is well to keep in mind possible qualifying factors—first, that a living snake invariably looks much larger than it actually is. Second, that it is virtually impossible to skin a snake without stretching its skin, and extremely difficult to determine the exact measurements of any snake more than 15ft in length. Trophy hunters indeed offer so much per foot of skin, which encourages the Indians, who capture most large snakes, to do some additional stretching. Third, that the deliberate faking of measurements, of which

F

there has been plenty, has damaged the credibility of genuine records. Manciet, for example, saw a faked photograph in a Manaos shop in which a group of men appeared beside a monster anaconda that would have measured 130ft long by 6ft diameter. To the eye of a professional photographer, the faking was immediately apparent. No less damaging are the lunatic-fringe tales—such as this account of the capture of a 32ft anaconda:

> Furiously the snake began to thrash about, and we expected to see the cage explode into kindling wood. The best way to quiet a snake is to feed it. Rod had a peccary among his specimens. The eighty-pound animal would just make a good mouthful for the anaconda. A half-hour later the anaconda was asleep with a huge bulge in its midriff.

It is not credible that a recently captured anaconda would take food in this way.

The fourth and last qualification is that though Theodore Roosevelt offered $5,000 for the skin and vertebral column, or either alone, of a snake measuring more than 30ft, this reward was never claimed. But to see a large snake in the wilderness is one thing. To kill it, secure it, and transport it intact through several hundred or thousand miles of ant-infested, ultra-humid jungle and down rivers abounding with rapids is quite another matter, whatever the reward for doing so.

Having made these qualifications, let us get down to fact or fiction. No one will dispute that acceptable measurements for a large anaconda are 15 to 25ft in length with a mid-girth of not less than 25in. Herpetologists have vouched for a specimen of 19½ft with a girth of 33in, and the largest killed by Fountain, though no doubt measured only roughly, was 24ft long and as thick as a man's body with a girth of 42in. Of other large specimens, Victor Norwood killed one of 25ft, and the largest measured by Leonard Clark was 26¾ft; while we have already referred to Schurz's stretched skin of 27¾ft, Up de Graff's estimate of 30ft, and to the unsubstantiated observation of a 37ft specimen by Gardner. To these may be added a large specimen encountered by my contemporary, Nicholas Guppy, on the Essequibo. This one was coiled on the top of a steep bank only a few feet from his boat. When Guppy shot at it, a dark patch appeared on its head and the vast spotted body relaxed. In comparison with the 17ft specimen he had shot a few months earlier he estimated it to be half as long again, and 8 or 10in in diameter, as against 6in: 'As its head touched the water the most horrifying transformation I have ever witnessed took place: the whole monstrous creature convulsed like a spring gone mad. Writhing, lashing, it tumbled into the river and out of sight. It would have uprooted a tree, crushed us all if it had struck us. We were aghast.'

It has been widely stated that the largest bona fide anaconda is the 33½ft captive in the Butantan Institute at Sao Paulo: but this is not correct, for two expert herpetologists—an American, Thomas Barbour and a Brazilian, Dr Jose Candido de Melo of the Rio de Janeiro zoo—have vouched for a 45ft skin; while Dr Afranio do Amaral, after examining the available evidence, is of the opinion that some anacondas may possibly exceed 45ft. There is also the statement of Lewis Gallardy, United States consul at Iquitos when Leonard Clark went up the Perene, that Peruvian skin traders, who brought in large numbers of skins every year to Iquitos, asserted that lengths of 40ft were frequently reached.

This brings us to the repeatedly ridiculed claims of Fawcett who, it may be recalled, was sent out, when a thirty-nine-year-old artillery officer, by the Royal Geographical Society to act as mediator in the 1906 frontier dispute between Brazil, Bolivia and Peru. With an international reputation as a boundary surveyor, Fawcett was unlikely to make gross mistakes in measurements of any objects; and notwithstanding his obsession with El Dorado, was most matter-of-fact in all his statements. Nowhere in his accounts of his travels does Fawcett exaggerate either the size or ferocity of any of the animals he encountered. Witness his sober statement, after he had been attacked by a bushmaster, that: 'It was quite nine feet long and about five inches thick, and the double fangs, if in proportion, would be over an inch. Experts claim that these animals reach a length of fourteen feet, but I have never seen one so big.'

It was in January 1907, at Yorongas, a remote settlement of two or three rubber-tappers' sheds, not far from the source of the river Acre, that Fawcett first heard rumours of gigantic snakes, when the manager of the *barraca* told him he had killed a 58ft anaconda on the Lower Amazon. This was followed by his own encounter with a colossal anaconda on the Rapirran. His description of this encounter in *Exploration Fawcett* is well known, but for our purposes is worth studying again:

> We were drifting easily along on the sluggish current not far below the confluence of the Rio Negro when almost under the bow of the *igarite* there appeared a triangular head and several feet of undulating body. It was a giant anaconda. I sprang for my rifle as the creature began to make its way up the bank, and hardly waiting to aim smashed a .44 soft-nosed bullet into its spine, ten feet below the wicked head. At once there was a flurry of foam, and several heavy thumps against the boat's keel, shaking us as though we had run on a snag.
>
> With great difficulty I persuaded the Indian crew to turn in shorewards. They were so frightened that the whites showed all round their popping eyes, and in the moment of firing I heard their terrified voices begging me not to shoot lest the monster destroy the boat and kill everyone on board, for not only do these creatures attack boats, but there is also great danger from their mates.
>
> We stepped ashore and approached the reptile with caution. It was out of action, but shivers ran up and down the body. As far as it was possible to measure, a length of forty-five feet *lay out of the water*, and seventeen feet in it, making a total length of sixty-two feet. Its body was not thick for such a colossal length—not more than twelve inches in diameter—but it had probably been long without food. I tried to cut a piece of the skin, but the beast was by no means dead and the sudden upheavals rather scared us. A penetrating, foetid odour emanated from the snake, probably from its breath, which is believed to have a stupifying effect, first attracting and later paralysing its prey.
>
> Such large specimens as this may not be common, but the trails in the swamps reach a width of six feet and support the statements of Indians and rubber pickers that the anaconda sometimes reaches an incredible size, altogether dwarfing that shot by me. The Bra-

zilian Boundary Commission told me of one they had killed in
the Rio Paraguay exceeding eighty feet in length! In the Araguaya
and Tocantins basins there is a black variety known as the Domi-
dera, or 'sleeper', from the loud snoring noise it makes. It is
reputed to reach a huge size, but I never saw one.

To my mind this is a perfectly straightforward account, marred
only by the reference to the paralysing effect of the snake's
odour; and note Fawcett's very modest estimate of a diameter
of not more than 12in, equivalent to a circumference of only
38in. Agreed, that a monster anaconda, still exhibiting reflex
actions, would be a difficult subject to measure with any
accuracy: but allowing Fawcett the generous error of 6ft on
that part of it out of the water, and a similar error on that in the
water, 50ft of anaconda is left. For that matter, one might
equally well suggest that Fawcett could have under-estimated.

Consider now another discredited account by Algot Lange,
whose two books on his experiences on the Amazon show him
to have been a careful observer. Like Fawcett, he heard of the
existence of giant snakes before he actually encountered one
himself. This was in 1910, when he was at the rubber station of
Floresta on the Javari, south-east of Iquitos, and talked with a
seringuero who, when canoeing past a creek, was impelled by
some inexplicable force, which he was unable to resist, to paddle
ashore. According to his story, which Lange was unable to
shake, he could not move from this place and became hysterical.
However, his cries were heard by three of his fellow workers
who, on paddling inshore, saw a gigantic anaconda coiled only
a few feet from him. After shooting it they measured its length
to be seventy-nine 'palmas'—the spread between thumb and
little finger—which Lange adjudged to be 52¾ft. Its circumference was eleven palmas, or more than 7ft.

Shortly after this, Lange was travelling by moonlight on the
Javari when one of his crew spotted a large anaconda half hidden
by dead branches on a sand-bar:

> Running the canoe ashore, I beheld a somewhat cone-shaped mass
> about seven feet in height. From the base of this came the neck
> and head of the snake, flat on the ground. We had stopped at a dis-

tance of about fifteen feet from him. The snake still made no move, but in the clear moonlight I could see its body expand and contract in breathing; its yellow eyes seeming to radiate a phosphorescent light.

Having killed the anaconda with pistol and Winchesters, Lange and his Indians camped for the night. The next morning they stretched its body out along the sand-bar:

> I proceeded to take measurements and used the span between my thumb and little finger tips as a unit, knowing that this was exactly eight inches.
>
> Beginning at the mouth of the snake, I continued to the end and found that this unit was contained eighty-four times. Thus 84 times 8 divided by 12 gives exactly 56 feet as the total length. In circumference, the unit was contained 8 times and a fraction, around the thickest part of the body. From this I derived the diameter 2 feet 1 inch.
>
> These measurements are the result of very careful work. I went from the tail to the nose over again so as to eliminate any error, and then asked the men with me also to take careful measurements in their own manner, which only confirmed the figures given above.

After skinning this anaconda and preparing it with arsenical soap, it measured when dried 54ft 8in, with a width of 5ft 1in. Although it was crated in preparation for shipment to New York, it apparently never arrived there, or subsequently disappeared; for although Blomberg made enquiries about it, none of the museums he contacted had any knowledge of it.

Consider also Up de Graff's encounter with a colossal anaconda on the headwaters of the Yasune, bearing in mind his long and practical acquaintance with every aspect of jungle life on the Amazon:

> Ten or twelve feet of it, covered with butterflies and insects of all sorts, lay stretched out on the bank in the mud; the rest of it lay in the clear shallow water, one huge loop of it under our canoe, its body as thick as a man's waist. It measured fifty feet for a certainty, and probably nearer sixty feet. Our canoe was a twenty-four footer; the snake's head was ten or twelve feet beyond the

bow; its tail was a good four feet beyond the stern; the centre of
its body was looped up into a huge S, whose length was the length
of our dugout, and whose breadth was a good five feet.

I called out to Jack to shoot. He reached out for his weapon,
but the noise he made in fumbling for it among the stores
alarmed the snake. With one great swirl of the water that nearly
wrecked us it vanished. The agility with which it moved was
astounding in view of its great bulk.

Now, you may consider Fawcett to have been a romancer and
Up de Graff to have exaggerated in the excitement of the encounter, but it would be difficult to fault Lange's methodical
measurements, which involved him in eighty-four hand-spans
from jaws to tail, and then a further eighty-four in reverse. Even
if he is credited with an over-estimate of 1in in every span, 49ft
of anaconda still remains.

So much for the 'fifty-footers'. Now let us turn to reports of
very much larger specimens. As reputable a naturalist as Alfred
Wallace considered it worth putting on record that there was a
general belief in Amazonia that anacondas reached lengths of
from 60 to 80ft; while Fawcett was informed that tracks of
snakes up to 80ft in length had been seen in the Beni swamps of
Madre de Dios. One may well ask how the track of a snake is
measured: but nevertheless this recalls an old account by a
Jesuit, Father M. C. de Vernazza who, when writing of his
mission to Zaparos in 1845, stated that:

> The Indians of this region have assured me that there are animals
> of this kind here of three or four yards diameter (*circumference*),
> and from thirty to forty long. These swallow entire hogs, stags,
> tigers and men, with the greatest facility; but it moves and turns
> itself very slowly on account of its extreme weight. When moving,
> it appears a thick log of wood covered with scales, and dragged
> slowly along the ground, leaving a track so large that men see it
> at a distance and avoid its dangerous ambush. That which I killed
> from my canoe upon the Pastaza (with five shots of a fowling
> piece) had two yards of thickness (*dos varas de grosor* not *de
> diametro*) and fifteen yards of length.

There is also the claim by a Campa Indian to have paced off the

body of an 8oft snake, and another by a Father Averico Vil-
larego to have photographed an anaconda on the Putamayo that
was 85ft in length. However, as the latter stated that this monster
had a girth of 31ft, his record must be dismissed out of hand—
unless, of course, this was an error in translation of the *dos varas
de grosor* type, for a diameter of 31 *inches* would be proportion-
ately correct for an 85ft snake. But consider the testimony of
another Jesuit long resident in Amazonia, Father V. Heinz:

> During the great floods of 1922, on May 22 at 3 o'clock to be
> exact, I was being taken home by canoe on the Amazon from
> Obidos; suddenly I distinctly recognized a giant water-snake at
> a distance of some thirty yards. To distinguish it from the
> *sucuriju*, the natives who accompanied me named the reptile
> *sucuriju gigante*, because of its enormous size.
>
> Coiled up in two rings the monster drifted quietly and gently
> down-stream. My quaking crew had stopped paddling. Thunder-
> struck, we all stared at the frightful beast. I reckoned that its body
> was as thick as an oil-drum and that its visible length was some
> eighty feet.

On subsequently questioning his boatmen, Father Heinz learnt
that another *sucuriju gigante* had been killed south of Obidos
while swallowing a capybara, and when opened up had been
found to contain four more capybaras which, it will be recalled,
are when full-grown the size of small sheep and weigh up to
120lb.

Still more recently, Bernard Heuvelmans has given an account
in *On The Track of Unknown Animals* of the experience of Serge
Bonacase, who accompanied Raymond Maufrais on one of his
earlier expeditions. They were hunting capybaras in the swamps
between the Rio das Mortes and the Rio Cristalino when their
guide pointed out an anaconda asleep on a rise in the ground,
half hidden among the grass. Approaching to within 20yd of
the snake they fired at it several times, and although it attempted
to get away, in convulsions, they caught up with it after 20 or
30yd and finished it off. Only then did they realise how enormous it was. When they walked along the whole length of its
immense body it seemed as if it would never end. What im-

pressed them most was the great size of its head. In describing this to Heuvelmans, Bonacase stretched out his arms in front of him with his hands together, forming a triangle with 2ft sides and an 18in base. Since none of the party possessed a measuring instrument, one of them held a piece of string between the ends of the fingers of one hand and his shoulder to mark off a length of 1m, or possibly a little less. They measured the anaconda several times with this piece of string, invariably arriving at the same estimate that it was twenty-four or twenty-five times as long as the string, and therefore almost 23m (75ft) in length. The diameter of its coils they estimated to be almost 18in (equivalent to a very modest circumference of 56in); and its mid-body was so heavy that the entire party were unable to lift it. This was a very dark-brown specimen with almost black irregularly oval rings on its sides: in contrast to the one shot by Guppy, which was olive-green with oval black spots on its back and white-centred spots on its belly and sides.

Reports of still larger specimens must also be considered, when recalling that the legendary battle near Tabatinga on the Solemoes, or upper Amazon, is associated with an account of a 130ft anaconda. In 1954 a Brazilian army patrol claimed to have killed a snake 120ft in length at Amapa near the border with French Guiana; and there is also the statement by Paul Tarvalho, a former pupil of Father Heinz, that he saw an anaconda, which he estimated to be 150ft long, emerge from the water at a distance of 250–300 yd. Finally, in *The Leviathans*, Tim Dinsdale, the Loch Ness Monster specialist, discusses the origins of two photographs published in Brazilian and Argentinian newspapers purporting to portray two *sucuriju gigante* killed with machine-guns in 1933 and 1948. One of these, which was stated to have been shot while digesting a steer, whose horns protruded from its jaws, and towed into Manaos by a river tug, was reported to have measured 131ft in length and 31½in in diameter, and to have weighed 5 tons: its head being so heavy that four men were unable to lift it. The other was killed on the Abuna (the parent river of Fawcett's encounter with his 60ft anaconda) in west Brazil, and was stated variously to be 115ft or 147ft in length.

Although the origins of these photographs are uncertain, Father Heinz was assured that the negatives had not been tampered with, and Dinsdale concluded after careful examination that the newspaper pictures are genuine and probably unretouched, though in his opinion the Abuna photograph may be of a dead *sucuriju* floating belly up. He adds that in either case the reptile depicted differs from any known giant snake in its exceptionally large eyes and mouth, and in the fact that its rib structure is thickest at the sixth convolution and not at the normal fourth.

For the present, until more positive measurements are forthcoming, the existence of 100ft *sucuriju gigante* may be considered not satisfactorily proven, though Lorenz Hagenbeck, son of Carl, the animal collector, was convinced that such gigantic serpents did exist, after hearing from Father Heinz of his experience, and also that of a Franciscan Father Frickel, who was able to approach to within a few paces of the head of one which was lying out of the water and whose eyes were 'as big as plates'. Hagenbeck drew up a tentative description of *sucuriju gigante*— up to 130ft long; 8ft in circumference at its thickest; exceptionally large and luminescent eyes, appearing bluish at night. And with these specifications he might have included an exceptionally large head.

I submit that the available evidence confirms, rather than denies, the existence of gigantic reptiles, not necessarily all of them anacondas, reaching lengths of 80 ft or more. One might add that since in Paraguay and adjacent territories there is a small race of anaconda (*Eunectes notacus*), there is no reason why there should not be extra-large races in other regions. The Indians on the Rio Cauceya told Blomberg that the La Apaya marshes were a centre for large *güio* (anacondas), and Blomberg himself captured one measuring 23ft there. It is perhaps significant that these Huitoto Indians were (uncharacteristically) terrified of the *güio*, and reported that one of their number had been attacked and engorged while fishing in the marshes two years before Blomberg's arrival. Guppy noted that the Kassikaitu river and its neighbour the Kinguwini, to the west of the Essequibo, and the swamps between the two rivers, have always been famed for the exceptional size of their anacondas and observed to be so by every European traveller since Schomburgk in 1837. Such concentrations of large snakes in certain districts can be paralleled by similar regional concentrations of large iguanas and caimans.

We cannot conclude this discussion on gigantic snakes without asking whether South American jungles and swamps also harbour living reminders of prehistoric areas. Since hundreds of thousands of square miles of jungle are still unexplored, who can state categorically what may, or may not, live in those unexplored areas of the Mato Grosso in particular, but also those of Colombia, Guyana and the Cordillera of the Andes, known only to a few tribes of Indians? Who knows what animals are to be found at the sources of the Orinoco in Venezuela, where among the almost impenetrable jungle of the Gran Sabana tower the 20-miles-long limestone plateaux and canyons of the *mesas*, empounded against the outside world by sheer cliffs from 3,000 to 10,000ft high? The Taurepan Indians knew of the Gran Sabana's great waterfall, with its single drop of over 3,000ft on the 5,000ft wall of the Augan Tupui, at the time of the Spanish Conquest: yet the existence of this highest waterfall in the world only became known to outside sources through the fortuitous observation of an aeroplane pilot.

We may agree with one zoologist that the conception of dinosaurs still surviving in Conan Doyle's 'Lost World' of the *mesas* does not bear serious consideration; but we may also agree with another zoologist that no one can say for certain that *Toxodon*, the guinea-pig as large as a rhino, no longer browses in the fastness of the Mato Grosso. I think we are justified in going further than this and asserting that it is probable, rather than improbable, that such unexplored regions contain certain mammals and reptiles still unknown to science, even if these be no more unusual than the large black bear that is reported from time to time in the eastern Andes, and is not to be confused with the rather small spectacled bear, South America's only known species. Leonard Clark actually watched a very large black bear clawing apart an ants' nest in a rotten tree-stump near Sutsiki in northern Peru, and subsequently shot it when it was swimming across a river: but its body sank and was stripped by piranhas. The Campa Indians told him that it was known to them as the *milne*.

Clark also noted that large areas of Amazonia are still reported in Indian legend to harbour, or to have once harboured—not very long ago if Van Gennep is correct—animals resembling giant sloths, armidillos and anteaters; and when he went up the Perene in 1946 several tribes of Indians east of the Ucayali described to him colossal creatures that could have resembled the 80ft-long, 20-ton reptile *Diplodon*, which fed on aquatic plants.

One such unknown animal may have been the creature that the Swede, Harald Westin, saw when he was on the Marmore river in the Mato Grosso about the year 1933. He described it to Blomberg (who was as sceptical of gigantic snakes as of re-activated dinosaurs) as being like a distended greyish-coloured boa with a head like an enlarged alligator's. It was 20ft in length and moved clumsily and awkwardly on feet resembling those of a lizard. Although its eyes were no larger than those of a pig, they 'glowed scarlet' and made Westin shudder when the creature raised its head and glared at him: 'I felt as if all my energy, all my courage, was drained away by that cold, piercing look.'

When Westin fired at it, the bullet struck home with a clucking sound as when a stone hits a heap of manure. Not a sound came from the strange animal, which walked slowly away on its shapeless trunk in the direction of the river.

8

Supernatural Jaguars

The jaguar is as revered throughout South and Central America as the tiger is in Asia. Indeed, the jaguar's hold over men's minds and beliefs far surpasses in its universality that of the tiger and the inhabitants of India. Man's dread of the tiger is understandable, for in Asia large numbers of tigers lived in close contact with a teeming human population, and the scourge of the maneater was terrible enough in practice, but still more terrible in its effect on the apprehensive minds of men. But the jaguar, though a formidable beast of prey, is a comparatively inoffensive predator where man is concerned; while if jaguars were (and still happily are) numerous, men were not, and there has never been any history of man-eating in South America comparable to that of the tiger in Asia that could inspire widespread physical dread. From Mexico to the Mato Grosso, the universal dread of the jaguar is, and always has been, predominantly of a mystical nature: the dread, real or professed, of an animal possessed of supernatural powers—by day a jaguar, by night a man or *shaman* (medicine man).

And only now, as the temples and cities of Mexico, Yucatan and Peru are uncamouflaged year by year, after centuries of obscurity within the strangling mesh of tropical creepers and lianas, are we beginning to realise for how long and to what an extraordinary degree the *mystique* of the jaguar has embodied in the fervid imagination of every Indian people their fears of the peculiarly oppressive, mysterious and horrific nature of the South American jungle which contrasts, in the main, with the relatively dry and open jungle inhabited by tigers in India. Pay no attention to those few white explorers who have compared travel through South American swamps and jungles to walking through English woods and marshes. Their debunking has been prompted by literary or commercial motives. Men like Candido Rondon and Theodore Roosevelt were the bona fide explorers. On one occasion the latter followed the trail of two jaguars straight across a marsh for eleven hours. 'We were torn by the spines of innumerable clusters of small palms with thorns like needles,' he wrote. 'We were bitten by the hosts of fire-ants, and by the mosquitoes, which we scarcely noticed where the fire-ants were to be found, exactly as all dread of the latter vanished when we were menaced by the big red wasps, of which a dozen stings will disable a man.'

The Chavin-culture people of the northern Andes, 5,000–6,000 years ago, were sculpturing in stone jaguars and other symbolic figures, resembling those fashioned by the Maya long after them. Jaguars were perhaps never as common in Mexico as in parts of South America. Nevertheless the Olmeca, who inhabited the Tabasca and Vera Cruz jungles from 3000 to 1000 BC, were jaguar worshippers. They were more than worshippers. They were jaguar psychotics—deforming their heads in imitation of the great cat's flattened skull, and depicting the child-like or Mongolian faces of their images with feline mouths: the lower jaw brutally exaggerated. The tradition of jaguar worship continued as an important element in the religion of the Zatopecs of Oaxaca, who were contemporaries of the Maya. On the flattened summit of the hill above Oaxaca was the citadel of Cosijo, the Jaguar God. To the Aztecs this was the Hill of the Jaguar: to the Mixtecs and Spaniards, Monte Alban (the White Hill). Among the vast Mixtec treasury in one tomb on the hill were thirty narrow strips of jaguar bone exquisitely carved with mythological scenes and inlaid with minute pieces of turquoise.

During the Spanish oppression, jaguar worship was incorporated in the secret cult of the Nahualistas, who took their title from the Nahua or Jaguar people whose civilization preceded the Aztecs' in Mexico, and whose name is still the word for jaguar among the Sumu Indians of Nicaragua. The Nahualistas, who wore jaguar skins and were adorned with their claws and teeth, were ferocious ritual assassins comparable to the Leopard Men of Africa. Their cult still survives in the perhaps unwittingly ironic jaguar dances performed by some Indians during Catholic fiestas.

To the Maya of Guatemala, Honduras and Yucatan, the jaguar and the crocodile together supported the world, and jaguars were favourite subjects of Mayan artists. In their religion the Rain Gods of the Four Quarters were portrayed as jaguars; of the gods they painted or sculptured the jaguar was second only in importance to the plumed serpent, Kukulcan. (In Leonard Clark's opinion, most dragon-like features in Mayan motifs are not, in fact, 'plumed serpents' but accurate representations of the large local iguanas or *tolocs*, 4 or 5ft in length. These are still to be seen everywhere among the Maya ruins in Yucatan, especially in the early morning, basking in the first warmth of the sun.) At Quirijua on the Mantagna river in Honduras there is a Mayan megolith representing a jaguar; at San Sebastian, in Guatemala, a monolith of a crouching jaguar; around the immense ruins of the Temple of Jaguars at Chichen-Itza in Yucatan runs a sculptured frieze of jaguars holding human hearts in their talons, and of naked warriors tormenting jaguars and eagles by thrusting flaming torches at them. Here, also, is one of the world's most superb sculptures: a jaguar, 33in high and 12in across the back, lacquered bright red, but with menacing white stone teeth, ferociously glaring jade eyes and seemingly lashing jade-encrusted tail. Seventy-four circular inlays of apple-green jade represent the rosettes on the hide, while a plaque of mosaic turquoise on its flat back depicts the sacred serpent, clouds, rain and Earth.

'Still today', observes Starker Leopold, 'no animal is more talked about, romanticized and glamorised at Mexican campfires than El Tigre, as the Spaniards named the jaguar. His chesty roar in the night causes men to edge towards the blaze and draw their *serapes* tighter. It silences the yelping dogs and starts the tethered horses milling. In announcing its mere presence in the blackness of the night, the jaguar puts the animate world on edge.'

The haunts of Mexican jaguars are, as we have seen, in the foothills of the coastal jungles: rarely anywhere on the central plateau. Thus, in those regions where the Zatopeca cult of the jaguar was strongest in the past, so today its *mystique* still dominates the common people (even if in some parts it holds no more terror than does the were-jaguar invoked by Indian mothers as a bogey with which to scare their children): just as the rattlesnake is held in more than physical fear on those same plateau lands where the plumed serpent was formerly worshipped. Possibly the religious wars between the jaguar worshippers and the later serpent worshippers of Quetzalcoatl were responsible for vandalism of sculptures at La Venta and Tres Zapotes in southeast Mexico. In the Quintana Roo, votive offerings to the jaguar corn-gods or *balaams* are still tied to branches of trees, and Balaam is a surname current among the remaining Maya Indians. In the Guianas, the jaguar is the original ancestor of many of the tribes who claim an animal pedigree, and jaguars feature in many of their folk tales, often anthropomorphically, though not always as the villain of the story.

Some 3,000 miles to the south, at the springs of the Amazon in northern Peru, the cult of the jaguar was no less dominant. The *Royal Commentaries of the Yncas*, together with abundant pottery shards, stress the reverence shown to both jaguars and pumas in the idol worship not only of the Indian peoples the Incas enslaved from northern Chile to Ecuador, but also of pre-Inca peoples. There, for five centuries after AD 1000, the jaguar was identified with the creator god, Vivacocha, and with the moon or night, as opposed to the condor which was the emblem of the sun or day. The jaguar was therefore a participant in ritual ceremonial rites, and the dominant designs on the pottery of this period are of ferocious cat-gods or terrifying centipede gods—complex nightmarish combinations of man with jaguar or puma, condor or serpent. In many of the designs, observes R. N. Salaman, the head of the jaguar or puma, with mouth open and canines bared, has some symbolic significance; but in

some instances the symbolism is dropped and the jaguar is portrayed devouring his victim, who may be bound and helpless, awaiting his fate.

This is not the place to speculate as to why all the ancient and in many respects highly sophisticated, though priest-ridden civilisations of South America were, without exception, tortured, warped and sadistic; but one can conjecture that, since jaguar and snake cults were widespread throughout Central and South America, they must have derived from a common culture or religion. As new dating techniques are developed and new cities and temples retrieved from the jungle so, almost annually, the span of man's history in the Americas is pushed back several thousand years. A few years ago it was reckoned to reach back no earlier than 10000 BC. Today 30000 BC is considered more probable, with an engraving on a large bone from the bottom of what used to be Lake Texcoco in Mexico City provisionally dated at about 43000 BC.

Salaman, in his monumental but peculiarly fascinating study of such an improbable subject for romance as the potato, has gone so far as to suggest that the universal dread of the jaguar provides a basis for charting the migratory paths of the earliest colonisers of that area of South America which today comprises Colombia, Ecuador, Peru, most of Bolivia, and the northern part of Chile, all of which except Colombia were united under the Incas. He argues that if man came from the west by sea, then he would have known nothing of the jaguar or the boa, the potato or the coca plant, until he encountered them as he penetrated eastward. In that case one would not expect that the dread of the former and the use of the latter would be already characteristic elements in the social system of the coast at an early archaeological date as, in fact, they were. The evidence would seem to point rather in the opposite direction, supporting the theory that man reached the Peruvian area from the east. According to Prado, the geometrical tatoo designs used by the Yeomiabas Amazons are not only almost identical with those used by the Agmavoes of the Altiplano in northern Brazil and the Tianhuanaios around Lake Titicaca (whose Kena-Kena

G

dancers wear sleeveless jackets or 'cuirasses' of jaguar skins), but were also those used by the Mayas, the Aztecs and the Incas which, in their turn, resembled those used by the Egyptians in the days of the Pharoahs.

However that may be, among the Inca and pre-Inca peoples the cult of jaguar and puma was not monopolised (sadistically) by the priests and warriors, but entered into every household in the land as designs on pots for everyday use, with an open-mouthed jaguar and a potato 'eye' often associated in one motif —patently a fertility symbol. Salaman suggests that the jaguar's head and huge teeth may have strengthened the implications of a 'good' mouth represented by the 'hare-lip', which is a peculiarity of many pots with human heads composed of potato tubers. Moreover, if a potato eye be regarded as a mouth, and potato buds as teeth serrated like a jaguar's, and the value of the seed tuber be measured by the vigour of the buds, then the bigger and more prominent the teeth, the greater the promise of the crop to come.

Why should jaguars have achieved this extraordinary dominance in the minds and lives of so many peoples of widely differing cultures over so long a period? They must have had an extensive geographical range. Those peoples with whom they came into contact must have had suitably receptive religious or animistic beliefs, as has in fact been almost universally the case in South America. The physical nature of their habitat must have been of a kind to foster belief in their supernatural powers. And finally, they must have possessed special dramatic qualities as animals—that special quality found in all the large cats that exercises a peculiar effect on man, whether he be aboriginal or white hunter. Witness the inexplicable supra-sensory experiences of Jim Corbett and other hunters in India, either with tigers directly or through the medium of the aboriginal Gonds, summed up in the American hunter, E. Marshall's epitome to the Indian tiger: 'Unless I can make you believe that there is something practically supernatural about tigers, that they are not just common flesh and bone and striped hide, but a kind of symbol of the jungle, of the cunning and ferocity and in-

credible strength and beauty of raw Nature, there's no use your
going on with this tale.'

The Chavante Indian barbs his arrows with the eye-teeth of
a jaguar. Necklaces of jaguar teeth adorn the Tariano braves
when they feast at the Place of the Jaguar at Yawarete on the
upper Negro. Cofan Indians on the San Miguel wear necklaces
of eye-teeth on ceremonial occasions as Europeans wear medals,
and Blomberg was amused to see one Indian fingering admir-
ingly those of another member of the tribe who sported the
evidence of having killed thirty jaguars single-handed. Even the
nude Mojo Indian of the lower Amazon wears a jaguar tooth on
a string round his neck.

These are the hunter's actual trophies of the chase. But with
his prey he identifies himself:

> Come little sister, come! Our shoulders are covered with the teeth
> of the jaguar, who prowls through the forest at night—

sing the Jurapari Indians as they dance; and there are jaguars
among the masked Betoya dancers on the Papory river. Raymond Maufrais was present at a dance of the Karaja Indians on
the Rio das Mortes, when two hunters armed with richly
feathered spears set out, making a complete turn of the village,
while uttering contented little yelps. Then they faced two other
dancers who pretended to be a pair of jaguars. The hunters
mimed the supple feline behaviour of the big cats and in their
turn surprised the prey, who was reluctant to stay and fight.
Leaping and screaming, with sudden shudders that made the
strands of their masks shake, they showed their contempt for
the cowardly female who yielded step by step and finally turned
tail, while the male remained alone to face the danger and to
cover her flight. Then the male jaguar retreated in his turn, and
the hunters gave a long cry of victory before pretending to fight
another imaginary enemy that had suddenly appeared.

To the animistic Indian every object in Nature, both animate
and inanimate, houses a spirit. *Hamaro Kamungka turuwati*: Every
thing has a jaguar, is an Arawak saying. Arawak is itself derived
from *Aruwa* (jaguar): just as the original name of the Carib

people was *Carinye* (arising from a jaguar). The jaguar is therefore not only seen to be flesh and bone and spotted hide,
trophies of which can be taken and handled, but is equally
credibly known to be endowed with supernatural powers. The
Indian knows well the physical vegetable ingredients of the
deadly *urari* or *curare* poison with which he anoints his arrows
or darts, but the addition of a few jaguar hairs and other foreign
bodies to the brew gives insurance cover against the supernatural, too, and also serves the practical purpose of rendering
the thin poison viscous enough to adhere to arrow-heads and
dart-points. One cannot be too careful for, as Salaman expressed
it: 'Rivers ebb and flow, trees grow and fall, the sun rules by day
and the moon by night, by reason of the spirit beings that inhabit them; and the forest, above all, is alive with spirits, mainly
hostile.' Jaguars, and also pumas and anacondas, are not solely
animals capable of inflicting bodily harm but, equally, potent
spirits which can, and do, invade every aspect of the Indian's
life.

The Jivaros in the country of the Pongo de Manseriche on the
upper Maranon profess to fear two gods: Yacu-Mammam and
Chulla Chaquhikuna (the Odd-footed One). With one human
foot and one jaguar foot the latter may be compared to the
Chac Mool (Red Jaguar or Red Feet), the man-beast with
human face, but with claws in place of hands, of the Maya more
than a thousand years before their day. Chulla Chaquhikuna is
Lord of the Forest, and though he is never seen, the Jivaros
point out his tracks to the white man, despite the fact that being
expert hunters and woodsmen they must, as Up de Graff
recognised, be well aware of the real identity of the beast that
made the tracks. Nevertheless, they must reassure themselves
of the physical presence of this god, and when they encounter
these particular tracks, then any subsequent unusual event, such
as an abundance of game or the presence of dangerous snakes
or an unsuccessful brew of *curare*, is attributed to Chulla Chaquhikuna's influence.

Jaguar and *shaman* are one and the same being in the mind of
the Indian, and *Iya*, in fact, signifies either in all the Betoya

tongues. The *shaman* assumes the form of a jaguar while alive, wandering through the jungle by night and killing his enemies without being detected. When he dies, he is transformed into a jaguar, enjoying the best of both worlds. As the jungle Indian believes today, so the sophisticated Maya believed, with their twisted minds, that since jaguars dug up graves by night, then those men who despoiled graves were in reality jaguars. Likewise, an unusually bold jaguar or *kanaima*, as such a one is known to the Caribs of Surinam, must be possessed by the spirit of a warrior or cannibal who, in order to enjoy the same life after death, either assumes the shape of a jaguar or, alternatively, animates its body with his spirit. If a Guarayan hunter shoots a jaguar he immediately runs away from the kill, reports A. Metraux, so that he may not be overtaken by the jaguar's soul. If he wounds one, his soul becomes a jaguar, and he is served in isolation at the tribe's drinking bouts. So too, the Mojo Indians are so terrified of the jaguar's spirit that their *shamans* take advantage of this fear to obtain offerings of food from the tribesmen, though any Mojo who wounds a jaguar acquires high prestige and usually becomes a *shaman*. If he kills one he takes the name of the slain animal (revealed to him by a *shaman*), while all his personal belongings are exposed in front of his hut and are subsequently regarded as the jaguar's property. He must also observe special rituals and subject himself to a series of taboos, which include fasting, cutting off part of his hair, and secluding himself in the temple where jaguar heads are worshipped. The bodies of dead jaguars are not taken into the village, because of a belief that to do so will result in an epidemic, but are eaten on the river beaches at a feast of drinking and drum-beating that lasts for several days during which time the participants stay away from their village. One wonders what is a *shaman's* assessment of a jaguar's powers?

Clearly, the universal animism of Indian peoples throughout the Americas provided a fertile seed-bed for the growth of jaguar and snake cults; and this animism was fostered by the peculiarly hostile and primeval nature of the Central and South American jungles, with their vast swamps and morasses exhaling the sickeningly sweet, musky or putrid stinks of orchids and moon-flowers; their soaking humidity; their suffocating growth of trees and massed vines, lianas and parasitic creepers, smothering man beneath innumerable layers of greenery, and inhibiting all sunlight except for rare shafts slanting between the giant columns of the trees. In *The Amazon*, Emil Egli has analysed the effect of the jungle on man:

> One is dissolved in the steaming vapour. The conscious mind is extinguished. There is no cool of the night, no undisturbed sleep; one must always be on the alert, drawing on one's reserves of energy, so as not to succumb apathetically to the enervating heat. There is no frost, no dryness. Flowers and fruit hang side by side in the eternal present of the always green foliage. All climatic enemies of plant life are here excluded. It is the pulse of day and night that rules all.

In these jungles are myriads of the most pestilential and ferocious insects to be endured anywhere in the world. Julian Duguid has been laughed to scorn for entitling his book *Green Hell*: but he was by no means the first or only author to use this title, which can be traced at least as far back as *Inferno Verde* published in the early years of this century. And not only Amazonia and the Mato Grosso, but most of the Central and South American jungle *is* a green hell of biting, stinging, poisoning flies and *piumes*, leeches and above all ants, especially the pincered, inch-long *tocandeira* and the various species of 'fire-ants' whose bites make a man scream. Most of the world's several thousand species of ants inhabit Amazonia, and in certain areas their incessant attacks on all vegetable and animal life render these regions virtually uninhabitable.

Of course there are areas where insects, such as mosquitoes, are relatively scarce at certain seasons. Verrill, for instance, noted that the jungles of Central America and of the northern parts of South America were remarkably free from mosquitoes except in the swamps and the lowlands below the first rapids. But there are other areas, notably the great cataracts on the Esmeralda and the Orinoco and the Casiquiare linking the latter with the

Rio Negro, and the Argentinian and Paraguayan chacos, where they are concentrated in such numbers as to be unendurable.

Caspar Whitney, a hard-bitten explorer in many parts of the world and not one to stress everyday hardships, had never suffered such torments from mosquitoes as on the Casiquiare and the upper Orinoco, where they formed dense clouds to a height of 6 or 8ft above the water. To Cherrie, with his vast experience of South American exploration, the Pilcomayo was the *Inferno*: 'I have never been in a locality where there were, day and night, such swarms of insect pests—mosquitoes, black flies, sand flies and *tabanos*; in the bushes and forest shade mosquitoes swarmed in such incredible numbers that they had to be brushed aside before one could aim a gun!' 'I have never spent a day on the Amazon or any of its tributaries,' declared Fountain, 'in which I was not at some hour, or at all hours, of the twenty-four driven to a desperation verging on lunacy by the attacks of mosquitoes.' The truth is that one cannot talk about the Amazonia jungle as one entity. It is not a single thing. It is a composite of thousands of jungles as alike and as different as the poles of the earth. Each man generalises from his own experiences in his own little part. And, by and large, the areas of Amazonia which man has subjected are tiny dots in a wilderness the size of Europe; the rest is ruled by the insect world.

Contemplate the overwhelming isolation of the hundreds of small tribes and sub-tribes of Indians, few of them numbering more than a score or two of men, women and children, scattered thinly through these inconceivably immense forests and swamps. (By 1958 the Indian Protection Service had classified 235 distinct tribes in Amazonia, and was aware of the existence of a further fifty or more.) To the commuter in his trans-continental plane, observes Bertrand Flornoy, cities such as Belem and Manaos and Iquitos appear as mere clearings in the forests, while the Indians' settlements are invisible; for in South America the jungle has always conquered man, not man the jungle, constantly opposing man's efforts with its irresistible power which transforms all decay into new life in a matter of hours. A path is no sooner opened than the jungle closes it. In the words of Emil Egli, again:

> Nowhere are birth and death so continuous and incessant. Hesitantly, as it were their funereal dance, the leaves fall from the trees to add to the rotting floor. The sap rises—there must be unimaginable streams of sap—from the roots to nourish this forest ocean, to extend its sway and to intertwine it together. From earth to life, from life to mould, from mould to earth and from earth again to life, the circle of nature is so vast that it baffles the mind.

And then, to the spirit-ridden Indian, there are the mysterious and inexplicable sounds that come out of the jungle, and even out of the rivers, for sometimes at sunset, wrote A. Fiedler in the *River of Singing Fish*, melodious sounds, like the clanging of bells, are heard coming from the water. This is a kind of sheath-fish, actually singing in the Ucayali: 'I heard it for the first time on a late afternoon when the sun was setting with unusual splendour and a tempest was blowing up. The forest and the river were calm. Then suddenly the sound of a bell jingled out of the deep water, first one bell, then two, and soon there arose the sound of many bells as if in chorus.'

The thin high whine of countless myriads of mosquitoes is always with the Indians, as is the clicking cacophony, like a million castanets, of the cicadas, and the drum-booming ululation of phosphorescent frogs. To Nicholas Guppy the jungle night was full of noises:

> As the sounds of day withdraw, a finer web of vibrations presents itself, like that in a sea-shell held against the ear: tiny constant rustlings, cheepings, pipings, hissings, indicating the myriad small life of the forest—the insects and worms and frogs—the rare cries of night birds and animals, and the never-ceasing rain of solid particles—leaves, twigs, fruits, fragments of bark, petals; falling, drifting, sinking, precipitating down through the many layers of leaves to the floor of the jungle. Sometimes larger objects drop with a startling thump; sometimes some creature moves stealthily through the forest—never is the forest quiet, yet its sounds have about them the quality of silence.

But it is a silence which may be haunted by the prolonged,

melancholy and almost human call of the *potoo* owl, the Mal de Lua; or the trembling wail, lost in a whisper, of the *halawoe* or poor-me-one, that large nightjar whose eyes glow like iridescent globes; or, dreaded by the Indians above all other sounds, the shrill diabolical screams (resembling those of the trumpeter bird) of the *warracaba*—jaguar spirits hunting through the jungle in packs of a hundred—perhaps identifiable with wild dogs or possibly, as Beebe has suggested, with the giant otters that inhabit the 'back water' of slow-flowing reaches of the Amazon and Orinoco and associated creeks and lagoons. Known to grow to lengths of 7ft and possibly half as much again, their coughing and gasping sighs make the hair creep on a man's nape. The Indian's jungle hides mythical beasts as real and credible to him as flesh-and-blood jaguars and anacondas: especially the fox-sized *carbunclo* with long black hair which, nevertheless, is only visible at night when it slinks slowly through the thickets and, if followed, opens a flap or valve in its forehead, from beneath which a brilliantly dazzling light issues—from a precious stone, says the Indian. Attempt to seize it, and you will be blinded before the flap is closed and the *carbunclo* disappears into the night. Possibly this mythical beast has a basis for reality in the *mitla*—half dog, half cat—which Fawcett reported to be black and about the size of a foxhound, though unlike any other animal he had seen; and which has not apparently been seen by any other white man.

But the jungle's hostility to man is sensed not only by the native Indian, but by all who hack their way through it, whether they be the inhumanly brave, barbarously merciless Conquistadores; or those African slaves, the Djukas, who escaped to the bush in the seventeenth and eighteenth centuries, though restricting their settlements to clearings along the river banks; or the wretched *caboclos* and rubber-gathering *seringueiros*, whose solitary tattered huts of bamboo and palm leaves are strung intermittently in minute clearings at the river's edge along 2,500 miles of the Amazon, and along countless tributaries, some unnamed on any map.

Its hostility has been perceived by legions of adventurers and by transient explorers like Duguid who, in describing his experiences with Sacha Siemel in the Mato Grosso jungle, wrote:

> During the next seven months I began to know the forest, and to understand the fiendish, callous power that underlay the calm exterior. Under the shadow of the leaves I was tired, elated, thirsty, hungry and unafraid. The silence of the forest is alert, watchful, awake. It is the silence of the tiger's paw; the silence of the darting bat; the silence of the snake. It is not a bit restful, nor does it indeed sleep. Rather it brings out all that is self-protective in a man.

Or, if you were a poet, like Jose Eustachio Rivera, then (as Gordon Meyer has translated him) the jungle is the:

> Croaking responseries of hydropic toads, the stagnation of putrified springs. Here the aphrodisiac parasite that covers the ground with dead bees, the abundance of obscene flowers contracting with sexual palpitations, drugging one with their sickly odours; the malignant liana, whose fuzz blinds animals. Here, at night, unknown voices, phantasmagorical lights, funereal silences. Death passing, giving light. The crepitations of jaws which devour for fear of being devoured. And when dawn sheds over the forest its tragic glory, there begins the outcry of those that have survived.

9

Hunting the Jaguar

By a curious duplicity in the mind of the Indian, the belief that a jaguar is a god, or *shaman*, possessed of supernatural powers in no way inhibits him from hunting it as an ordinary beast of the chase. Indeed, the traveller would be hard put to find any Indian tribe from Mexico to the Gran Chaco which was not in possession of jaguar skins and necklaces of jaguar teeth. However, Indians find it advisable to take certain precautions before setting out on a jaguar hunt. Those in the Guianas, for example, place implicit faith in the potency of *beenas*. These are usually obtained from such plants as *caladiums* with arrow-shaped leaves, which are planted near their settlements; though sometimes from other sources such as the musk-gland of a peccary or the mucus of a live frog or the ashes of a burnt one. To each animal its special *beena*: in the case of a jaguar a *caladium* with variegated red and white spots. A *beena* inspires the Indian with confidence in his hunting, and its properties are exploited by rubbing the acrid juice of its bulb or tuber into incisions (taboo lines) about the mouth or on chest or arms. Those tribes, such as the Wai-Wai, who use hunting dogs, rub the *beena* into a cut on a dog's nose; and since each dog, or pack of dogs, specializes in hunting a particular animal, the appropriate *beena* must be employed. The simple savage! The more 'primitive' a people the more complicated, it seems, their everyday life. No 'civilised' man could support the nervous strain of such a complexity of taboos and spirit fears.

Man has hunted jaguars, and taken them alive in empty or staked pits from the earliest times, for the dungeons in which the

Incas punished those convicted of treason or disobedience, held
jaguars (and also pumas and bears). In the *Royal Commentaries
of the Yncas* we read that when Pizaro's ship arrived at Tumbez:

> There was some hesitation as to landing among a hostile people,
> and a Greek named Pedro de Candia volunteered to go first.
> Putting on a coat of mail reaching to his knees with a sword by
> his side and a cross in his hand, he walked towards the town with
> an air as if he had been lord of the whole province. The Indians to
> find out what manner of man he was let loose a lion [puma] and a
> tiger [jaguar] upon him, but the animals crouched at his feet.
> Pedro de Candia gave the Indians to understand that the virtue of
> the cross he held in his hand had been the cause of this miracle.

As late as the 1920s, MacCreagh observed the Tucana Indians on
the Tiquie tributary of the upper Negro trapping jaguars with
self-baiting poles set up near the village hen-house; while about
the same time C. W. D. Fife found that the Turas, in order to
avoid damaging the skins, trapped jaguars in grass-root snares
hung from trees across tracks leading to rivers or water-holes,
and arranged pulley-wise with a running-noose in such a
fashion that a snared jaguar hung itself. The Turas are one of
the few tribes that do not use jaguar skins for decoration or
clothing, but as rugs in their palm-thatch huts or as waterproofs
against torrential rains. Another are the Locandons—a dying
Maya tribe of the Chiapas—who, though hunting jaguars extensively with their small breed of dogs, barter their skins for salt.
According to Prado, snaring and baiting are still regularly employed in Amazonia, though a jaguar has such an extraordinarily acute nose that neither method is very successful. He adds
that it is almost impossible to track and follow a jaguar because
it moves so swiftly and stealthily, covering as much as forty
miles through the jungle in a night.

Although von Tschudi had reported, early in the nineteenth
century, that the majority of the Indians in Peru dreaded jaguars,
they nevertheless hunted them with dogs and killed them with
spears or arrows or blow-tubes—as the Cofan Indians still do.
G. F. Masterman, twenty years later, was impressed by the
extraordinary courage displayed by some Indians in Paraguay

in attacking jaguars of the largest size, though armed only with a knife and a poncho as a shield:

> Two men usually went together, with a few yelping curs to bring the tiger to bay. Then one of the men, rolling his woollen poncho over his left arm and with his long, keen-pointed knife in his right hand, met the infuriated animal as he made his spring, and drove his weapon between the vertebrae of its neck, generally with un-erring aim. Should he miss, his companion comes to his assistance, and in a moment the huge brute would lie disabled at their feet. But the more usual mode of destroying them was catching them in large wooden cages, like an old-fashioned rat-trap, and then killing them by a thrust with a lance.

When Henry Rusby was in Bolivia in 1885 he encountered a native jaguar hunter in the *cinclona* region of the Mapiri whose weapon was a long, straight, two-edged sword held in his right hand, while his left arm, heavily swathed with tough bagging material, served as a shield. Having attracted the attention of the jaguar, he would advance towards it, while at the same time endeavouring to infuriate it into springing at him and dis-embowelling itself on his sword. This method of killing a jaguar, or ones very similar to it, is evidently widely practised. In the Mato Grosso a jaguar is goaded into charging and impaling itself on a spear whose butt rests on the ground. Sacha Siemel claims to have killed many of his jaguars in thirty seconds with a similar technique acquired from a Guato Indian, after first baying them with dogs. He used a massive spear, 6 or 7ft in length, known as a *zagaia*, which had a second blade set across, and almost at right-angles to the shaft, near its point. When the jaguar sprang at him from a distance of 10 or 15ft and impaled itself on the point of the spear, the cross-piece prevented it from clawing its way up the shaft and reaching him with its talons, and also provided Siemel with leverage as he sought to work the blade into its heart.

Siemel killed all his jaguars single-handed, shooting most of them within a range of 20ft (in some instances with bow and arrow), but also spearing many, often after running them for several hours with his three or four dogs through the terrible country of the Xarayes marshes. Mechanic, hunter extraordinary, animal collector, explorer, photographer, linguist, philosopher—reading Tolstoy, Gogol and Victor Hugo during his siestas—Sacha Siemel was a very hard case (perhaps he still is, for he was born in 1890, emigrating to South America in 1907), yet at the same time in love with his wilderness and tenderhearted enough to weep when his foremost hunting-dog was finally killed by a jaguar. It is a tragedy that, unlike Jim Corbett in India, he has not apparently left us any personal record of his fifty years' (or more) experience of the Mato Grosso and its fauna; though, in *Tiger Man*, Julian Duguid presented a semi-fictional biography of his life up to the early 1930s.

Victor Norwood has given a highly-coloured account, as recently as 1964, of a jaguar hunt by Macusi Indians on the Japura river:

There was a water-hole fed by a stream flowing through a ravine where jaguars lurked during the night to make their kill when other creatures came to drink. It was agreed that we try this area first. When I proposed digging a pit and baiting it with the carcase of some creature, and then concealing it with branches, Jefferson smiled. The Macusi would tackle jaguars with nets and ropes, he said. Usually they speared marauding jaguars, but he would give instructions that in this instance no man must kill or harm a jaguar unless such a move was essential to his safety.

Shortly after daybreak a noisy group of Macusi gathered outside the bungalow. Most of them carried coils of tough creeper rope in addition to spears, machetes, and bows. A few had large nets. The gorge proved to be a perfect haven for jaguars. It was choked with brush and rank vegetation. There was barely enough light to reveal the track as we paused at the entry to the ravine.

A few Macusi armed with spears entered the tangle from the farthest approach and began to beat their way towards us while other Indians waited with ropes coiled and nets poised on light-weight pole frames.

Presently we became aware of movement among the undergrowth, of grunts and low, coughing snarls . . . two magnificent jaguars quitted the ravine together and streaked past the waiting Indians. One fouled a net and was bowled over, raging in baffled fury. The other avoided the snare and sprang with appalling swift-ness at a young Macusi's throat. The latter sank quickly to one knee, placed the butt of his spear against the ground, and calmly waited for the beast to impale itself on the formidable point. The jaguar's weight and impetus snapped the spear shaft, and a slashing paw caught the Macusi a glancing blow as he rolled aside. His chest was torn, but despite spurting blood and strips of peeled skin he didn't utter a sound; he merely clambered up and reached for another spear. . . .

Several more animals broke cover, including a number of jaguars, one of which avoided a net only to be snared by the loop of a rope . . . two Indians quickly tossed a mesh over the squalling cat, and we had another fine specimen for our zoo collection. No fewer than four jaguars then slunk from the brush simultaneously, hesi-tated, but were reluctant to turn back towards the source of weird calls and the shrill notes produced by bird-bone flutes. Two charged, and were promptly speared. One, a handsome animal with a trace of white under its lower jaw, crouched for a moment, then launched its sinewy length at me. I was obliged to shoot. An Indian succeeded in netting the fourth beast.

The beaters emerged from the ravine, and we thought the hunt was over. But as we were transferring the snared cats into strong, pole cages, a lone jaguar appeared above us on the gorge rim, stood for a while in plain view, then slunk away. However, soon afterwards it reappeared among brush near the ravine entrance. When some of the Macusi started towards it the brute disappeared again. On our way back to the settlement we glimpsed this jaguar several times. For the first time we realised that it was a female, and she seemed to be trailing us. Out of curiosity we set down the cages with their snarling occupants, and concealed ourselves to see what the female would do, and if we could determine what it was she was after.

Presently she emerged from a cane brake beside the track and padded close to the nearest cage, sniffed around it, then reared up and clawed at the poles as if trying to release the great beasts prowling inside. She bit the tough wood and gnawed at the lash-ings until we considered it advisable to intervene. When we showed ourselves, instead of making off the cat stood her ground defiantly. And when we started towards her, she commenced a slow stalk towards us, with tail lashing and yellow fangs bared. I prevailed on a couple of Macusi to cast a net over her. No sooner was she in the cage with her male consorts than she settled down to a process of licking their glossy hides, seemingly untroubled by her confined surroundings.

Both Indians and ranchers have always employed dogs when hunting jaguars, primarily in order to drive them out of the jungle into more open country, where they can be despatched more easily or, as in the Guianas, lassoed; though on the Nayarit coast of Mexico dogs are used to drive both jaguars and ocelots through the swamps towards gunners in boats. Guppy recounts an interesting conversation with one of his men about the Yawarda dogs, concerning the chief's statement that those used for hunting jaguars must have long tails. A dog with a short tail would always be killed, because when the jaguar sprang it would jump backwards and hit a tree or get itself tangled up in lianas: whereas a long-tailed dog would use his as an 'antenna', feeling behind it all the time for a clear way to escape.

This recalls Fawcett's reference to the double-nosed Andean tiger-hound, which he saw only at Santa Ana on the Marmore river in the Bolivian Chaco. This dog's two noses were as cleanly divided as if cut by a knife, and the breed was highly valued for its acute sense of smell and ingenuity when hunting jaguars.

On many large ranches a *tigrero*, or tiger hunter, is still a regular employee. With his small pack of mongrels or terriers he may trail a cattle-killer for many days, until it eventually retreats into a thicket; but while one hunted jaguar may allow itself to be bayed by dogs and then charge them, another will climb a tree and sit there, calm and unconcerned, beyond the reach of the dogs. This is confirmed by Siemel's Guato-Indian instructor in the art of spearing, in whose experience a hunted jaguar roared only when at bay on the ground, while seven out of ten would climb a tree. S. P. Young, however, found that since hunted jaguars were faster than pumas, not so easily winded, and possessed greater endurance over a long run, they did not tree as readily as pumas when close-pressed.

On the cattle plains of the Beni, where jaguars were very numerous at one time, Fawcett noted that they were not con-

sidered particularly dangerous and were generally hunted by
two men working together on horseback with lassoes; and Hudson was told of a pampa jaguar which, hunted in this way, sought
refuge in a dense clump of dried reeds. There, since it could not
be lassoed, the reeds were fired. But, instead of breaking out,
the jaguar lay where it was with head erect, glaring at the men
through the flames, until lost to sight in the black smoke. Subsequently its charred body was found where it had last been seen.

Finally we may mention hunting methods based on attraction
rather than pursuit. The Sinoalese hunter takes up his position
in a male's territory after dark and simulates its roar. To this the
owner responds at any time of the year, and not only during
the mating season. E. W. Nelson describes how, in the Guerrero
district of Mexico, the male jaguar commonly emerges from his
lair, located near the head of some small canyon in the foothills,
early in the evening and proceeds down the canyon, roaring at
intervals. On moonlight nights the native hunters place one
of their number, expert at imitating animal cries with a short
wooden trumpet, near the mouth of the canyon. As soon as the
jaguar roars, the trumpeter answers it at intervals, gradually
attracting the beast towards the waiting hunters.

Hans Gadow, who travelled through the southern parts of
Mexico in the early years of this century, refers to the use of a
deer's bone, 3in long and with a thin film pasted over one end,
as a simulator; though with this instrument the hunter imitated
the bleat of a hind or kid by sucking at the bone. The latter also
employed a lantern, both to illuminate the sights on the rifle and
to reflect in the jaguar's eyes. However, Gadow added that hunting jaguars with this technique was seldom successful. Yet another method of luring jaguars is practised by the Bororo Indians
when the cattle pastures of the Mato Grosso are flooded
during the rainy season. Under these conditions the Indians,
equipped with long spears and bark conches, paddle out in their
canoes. On a jaguar roaring from some tree-covered knoll protruding from the floods, a simulation of the female's mating call
is sounded on the conch. This attracts the male into the water,
and as it 'homes' on the call, the Indians paddle alongside and

H

spear it as they would a fish. Nicholas Guppy was shown by Indians in British Guiana how to produce an exact imitation of the jaguar's roar by rubbing the cut end of a small palm leaf against a cutlass blade, though if the angle between leaf and blade was not correct the knife-sharpening scream of the *caracara* hawk was produced instead.

10

Jaguars and Men

Jaguars have permanent relationships only with ranchers, herds-
men and gauchos because of their flocks and herds, and with
Indians because of their dogs and numerous tame animals.
Although Bates saw young jaguars running loose about the
houses of Brazilian villages, and Fawcett noted that quite a large
one was allowed to wander about a house near Rurenabaque on
the Beni, the jungle Indians who habitually tame and keep in
their settlements almost any animal one can name except possibly sloths, opossums and howler monkeys, do not include
jaguars in their 'menageries'. The toucan searches for bugs in its
master's hair. The curassow acts as rat-catcher, as does the boa in
the roof thatch. Peccaries and coatis wander in and out of huts at
will, following their owners to and from the forest, and sleep
on the hut's dirt-floor at night, or even in an Indian's hammock
to keep him warm. A capybara that, when young, had frolicked
in the water with the Indian children, remained tame when
fully grown and became extremely possessive, attempting to
drive away anyone who kept its master too long in conversation;
while a tapir, several years old, which lived near an Arawak
village on the Pomeroon river, was never harmed by the Indians
and occasionally called to see its former master.

Monkeys are whistled down out of trees; macaws and parrots
are stunned with arrows whose points have been blunted by
small discs, or are temporarily paralysed by slightly poisoned
blow-darts and revived with salt. The process of training is
simple and direct, says Guppy, and designed to produce rapid

submission: 'The animal is put in darkness, in a box or under a bowl, for a day or two without food or water. At the end of that time, if it is still alive, it is usually prepared to make friends. Its face is rubbed into its owner's arm-pits, or smeared with his red body-paint, so that it knows his smell. It is then released—nothing more. It may run away, but usually does not. And any creature that is naturally shy is given to as many people as possible to handle, so that it becomes accustomed to humans.'

Nevertheless baby creatures are treated with the utmost tenderness and care. Undoubtedly they help to satisfy the strong maternal yearnings of the frequently childless Indian women, and baby mammals may be suckled at the women's breasts. Schurz confirms this and points out that the Indian does not kill for the pleasure of killing but only for food, or to protect himself on those rare occasions when he is attacked by a wild beast: 'If he keeps a few chickens he will not kill the roosters, because he likes to hear them crow in the early morning.' The Indian, however, is not a potential member of the RSPCA. Although the birds are full-winged they seldom boast any tail or flight feathers because they are kept primarily as a perpetual source of supply for the braves' gorgeous head-dresses: just as the mammals serve in case of need as a reserve food supply. He may like to have these tame animals around: but he is totally unmoved by the sufferings of a pet deer with a broken leg being used for target practice by his sons with their bows and arrows.

So large a beast of prey as a jaguar would not be welcome as a 'pet' among the Indians, who have difficulty in providing themselves with sufficient meat, periodically hunting out all game within a week's distance from their settlements, and further straitened by the seasonal floods that prohibit both hunting and fishing. But jaguars are not untameable, as has been widely stated. They breed well in captivity, and more than a hundred years ago Lieut L. Gibbon noted that in Bolivia many gentlemen had tigers about their establishments. Though generally kept chained for fear of injury to strangers, they were docile and playful with acquaintances. Lieut Henry Lister Maw, twenty-five years earlier, had referred to a black jaguar, captured as a cub, which James Campbell, one of the earliest British residents in Para, kept in his house:

Its muscular power was extraordinary. It would frequently lie upon its back, with its head and all four feet turned upwards. On one of these occasions I was standing in a gallery, looking at it, when a terrier passed by. The tiger saw the dog and sprang at him directly from his back, apparently without turning. We were told of a circumstance when the tiger got hold of a pig and carried it off to its den. Every exertion was made to release the grunter, but in vain, until a Newfoundland bitch, of which the tiger had been afraid when young, was called. The bitch immediately rushed into the den, when strange as it may appear, the tiger offered no resistance, then threw himself on his back as if afraid, and the pig was rescued. This tremendous animal was confined only by a collar round the neck, and a chain not so stout as those I have known broken by Newfoundland dogs. His den was much like a dog-kennel, and was placed in the yard, through which people were constantly passing and repassing. What was most strange, the young men not infrequently amused themselves by kicking him, which to be sure produced no great sensation of pain on his part; if he got sulky he was broom-sticked. One night, after coming from a party, nothing would serve the young men but that they would take a candle and burn the tiger's whiskers or mustachios, which they did to his annoyance. The tiger was washed every morning by a negro, and appeared to like the water being thrown over him, his usual noise resembling the mewing of a cat, though not so loud.

The invasion of South America by Europeans, together with their stock, inevitably brought large numbers of jaguars into a much more extensive association with man than ever before, since domestic animals were so much easier to stalk and kill than wild prey. During the First World War, when the demand for meat led to an old cattle-trail being reopened through 180 miles of forest in British Guiana, large numbers of jaguars were attracted to the trail and made frequent attacks on the droves. Domestic stock were a particularly valuable source of food at those seasons when the vast floods characteristic of South American rivers obliged the jaguars to emigrate from their regular haunts.

Darwin, for example, recorded severe losses among cattle and horses when floods drove the jaguars from their islands on the Parana. Such forced or voluntary migrations from their home jungles on to the cattle savannas no doubt induced some jaguars to become confirmed cattle killers; and according to Sandeman, the cattle in the montana country to the east of the Mayo Bamba on the Amazon have to be penned at night because of the many jaguars in the surrounding forest. So too, G. M. Dyott found the Indians near Yurimagas in northern Peru rounding up their cattle and pigs into the plaza before dusk. However, in Leopold's opinion cattle killing is probably mainly restricted to individuals, because when these are shot the depredations cease, despite the continuing presence of other jaguars. When Gadow was at Tetela in southern Mexico he was told that jaguars never killed cattle or attacked the inhabitants because deer were plentiful in the forests on the slopes of the distant mountains, though they would break into the farm steadings at night in search of dogs and pigs. Yet during his stay at Motzorongo, a neighbouring sugar estate, a jaguar was killed while in the act of pulling down a cow near a house in broad daylight. Such a pattern of indivuality is also characteristic of cattle-killing tigers.

But once the habit is formed, then perhaps a jaguar may prey almost exclusively on cattle. Im Thurn recorded that hardly a night passed in Guiana when cattle were not attacked; and Schomburgk observed that the maintenance of fires around the fences of the cattle-pens on the Guiana ranches would by no means deter confirmed cattle killers. In the 1850s jaguars were reported to be so numerous on the Venezuelan *llanos* that it was impossible to rear cattle or horses. Brazilian ranches appear to have been especially plagued. We have already noted that Sacha Siemel killed more than three hundred cattle-jaguars on the ranches of the Xarayes, and in the early decades of this century the ranchers wlecomed him almost with tears of gratitude in their eyes, since a single jaguar was commonly believed to make a kill every five days, and there is every indication that they were extraordinarily numerous. During the course of eleven days hunting with Duguid in the Xarayes in 1931, for example,

Siemel speared seven jaguars, roped three cubs, and also shot two jaguars and a puma with bow and arrow. Another hunter, Pedro Pinheiro de Lemos, is also reported to have shot more than three hundred jaguars on the Fazenda ranch on the Araguaya.

Widespread cattle killing is not likely to be experienced in those regions abundantly supplied with natural game. Roosevelt mentioned that though he killed one large male jaguar, well-known as a cattle killer, on the Rio Taquari, in general only an occasional calf was killed, and only exceptionally would an adult male begin cattle killing, because there was an ample supply of capybaras, deer, and small caimans available: whereas in other districts at no great distance jaguars were reported to prey almost exclusively on cattle and horses, though avoiding large bulls and showing caution in attacking cows in a herd led by a bull.

Jaguars apparently prefer horses and mules or burros to cattle. On one ranch in the Mato Grosso, Roosevelt found that instead of killing cattle, jaguars were preying solely on mules; and it was Fawcett's experience that mules were more afraid of jaguars than of any other animal: the paw of a freshly-killed jaguar carried in the saddle-bags being more effective than any spur, though mules, unlike horses, do not panic and stampede when jaguars are about. Jaguars no doubt have difficulty in procuring prey in Yucatan's arid scrub jungle, and one of Leonard Clark's two mules was finally killed by a jaguar, which had trailed them for several days through the Quintana Roo jungle, moving in half-loops, keeping downwind, and patiently following the variable eddies of air, as Clark worked round and through the hills. His hunter told him that on one occasion in broad daylight a jaguar had actually leapt on the horse he was leading through the bush. 'The dread of jaguars hangs like a sword of Damocles over the head of anyone responsible for an expedition into the rain-forest,' wrote Wolfgang Cordan of the Locandon jungle in the extreme south-east of Yucatan. This partiality for horses reminds us that though there were no horses in South America at the time of the Conquest, there had been large indigenous herds at an earlier date, the causes of whose extinction are not known.

Domestic swine are naturally high among the jaguar's preferences, and easily obtainable when the half-wild sows go into the forest to farrow. In the Peruvian Pajonales, jaguars habitually came out of the forest into the plantations and villages, according to von Tschudi; and he recounts an amusing story of how:

> An Indian one night heard his only pig squeaking loudly, as if in pain. He hastened to the door of his hut to see what was the matter and discovered that an ounce had seized the pig by the head, and was carrying it off. The Cholo, who determined to make an effort to recover his property, seized the pig by the hind legs, and endeavoured to drag it from the grasp of the robber. This contest was kept up for some time, the ounce, with his eyes glaring in the darkness, holding fast the head of the pig, and the Indian pulling it hard by the legs. At length the Indian's wife came to the door of the hut with a lighted faggot, and the scared ounce, with terrible howlings, slowly retired to the forest.

Any domestic animal attracts a jaguar. Sir John Graham Kerr, for example, was standing on the banks of the Pilcomayo early one morning near his 'live meat', in the form of two sheep, when he was alerted by a faint sound, and saw a jaguar, looking gigantic in the faint light, advancing in great bounds; but, on Kerr running towards the jaguar and clapping his hands, it turned away and made off. But like the leopard, though unlike most tigers, a jaguar prefers a dog to any other domestic prey—a preference highlighted in Azara's no doubt apocryphal account of the jaguar (possibly a rabid individual) that carried off from a camp in the forest first a dog, then a negro, then an Indian, and finally a Spaniard! Schomburgk refers to jaguars seizing dogs from the interior of houses, and their liking for dogs is confirmed by both Blomberg and Guppy. The latter noted that the tribal houses at Yawarda (the most southerly village in British Guiana) in which the hunting dogs were tied up on shelves, 4ft above the ground, were built with strong walls of split *euperpe* stems as a protection against the incursion of jaguars.

The transitory camps of explorers and travellers are frequently visited by jaguars in the course of their perpetual quest for food. Many are extremely bold, and not to be deterred by large camp-fires—as Bates found when, although his men lit fires around his encampment at Ega because several jaguars were roaring a furlong distant, some approached to within 20yd of the camp while the men slept. So, too, at midnight, Waterton heard the soft tread of a jaguar approaching his camp on the Essequibo. The moon had gone down, but every now and again he caught a glimpse of it pacing to and fro by the light of the camp-fire. Whenever the fire died down the jaguar would approach a little closer, sometimes to within 20 yd, and sit back on its hind legs like a dog, though retreating abruptly when the fire was made up, and finally bounding away when his Indian companion let out a yell.

D. G. Fabre (the only white man to live, with his wife, among the parent tribe of the Chavantes) found the pug-marks of a jaguar stamped all over the tarpaulin covering his equipment at his Mato Grosso camp on the Araguaya; and this large beast was shot as it was about to drink from the river only a few yards from the camp-fire and the party's equipment and canoe. Camp-visiting jaguars are no doubt attracted mainly by the smell of meat. Fawcett, after shooting several *marimonos* (black spider monkeys), suspended their carcasses from high branches out of reach of any prowling marauders. Nevertheless, in the middle of the night he was awakened by a bump under his hammock, as though some heavy body had passed beneath it, and peering out he saw in the light of the moon the form of a large jaguar: 'It was after the monkey-meat, and had little interest in me, but in any case it would have been foolhardy to shoot in the uncertain light, for a wounded jaguar at close quarters is a terrible thing. I saw the beast raise itself on its hind legs and claw at a carcass. In the moment of grasping what it sought the rustle of my hammock disturbed it; it turned away with a snarl, bared its teeth, and next moment was gone as silently as a shadow.'

Wolfgang Cordan had a similar experience in the Chiapas:

Our hammocks formed a circle. In the middle of the night somebody pushed violently against Herminio's hammock, even touched his face.

'Who's that?' Herminio said, half asleep and not too pleased. 'Burrr,' said the tiger.

Herminio gave a yell and we all jumped out of our hammocks and listened. A twig snapped, then another. We lit up the wall of forest with our torches in one spot after another. Suddenly we saw him, not forty yards off: the tiger had turned his head to look into the light. With a bound he vanished into the undergrowth and kept on prowling round us. At four, just before dawn, he finally retreated. A tiger's hour is between one and three.

Schomburgk gives an amusing account of an incident at a Carib village on the Rupunini:

My brother's tent was pitched about 100 paces from the houses of the village. One of his sluts had a pup that was missing in the morning, and soon after a hammock, and so on each following night another piece, a cloth or a cooking utensil was gone. The robberies soon extended to the tents of his three European companions. The ferocious howl of the animal had naturally made the company cautious and my brother, while working in his tent late at night, just happened to look up from what he was doing, when he saw in front of him something that he could not quite make out, owing to the hammock having been already slung: he accordingly held up the light, only to recognize the jaguar standing four paces ahead calmly gazing into his eyes, but before he had time to seize the pistol his troublesome visitor had disappeared. Next night he was awakened from sleep by an animal that was just about creeping under his hammock and brushing its back up against his back: thinking it was one of his dogs, he gave it a sound slap— he did not hit the dog, but the jaguar which, with a growl, made a spring through the tent-wall. In the morning a general hunt was organised in the course of which, not the disturber of their peace, but certainly the stolen goods, down to a table-cloth, were found scattered through the brushwood.

Outside camp, there are incidental encounters, when a jaguar follows a man out of curiosity or mistaking him for prey. When G. H. H. Tate was collecting plants and small mammals on Mt Duida in Venezuela, its summit was reached by constructing a series of ladders leading from one ledge to the next up rather more than a vertical mile of forested slope; and his trackers established that one night a jaguar had ascended by these ladders, and after roaming over nearly five miles of their cut trail on the summit, had gone down again a little before sunrise.

Bigg-Wither was trailed by a jaguar, roaring intermittently, on the Parana; and Verrill and a companion were dogged by one for ten miles through the Panamanian jungle. Padding along some 30yd behind them, it retreated into cover whenever they retraced their steps, but made no attempt to close the gap when they broke into a run, and finally left them when they reached the first Indian house.

Verrill had a still closer encounter with a jaguar when hunting alone in a Costa Rica forest. Overtaken by a torrential downpour, he had sought partial protection between the hip-like roots of a huge tree. Placing his gun in a dry spot in the shelter of the broad leaves of a parasitic plant, he squatted down close to the roots and waited for the rain to cease. Presently he heard a rustling sound from behind the root beside him, but supposing it was merely some bird or lizard, took no notice of it until, when the worst of the shower was over, he got to his feet and casually glanced over the edge of the intervening root. To his astonishment he found himself face to face with a fully-grown jaguar snuggled against the opposite side of the root. Less than 3in of wood had separated them while they sheltered from the downpour. For a full minute they gazed at each other and then, with a lazy yawn, the jaguar stretched itself, rose slowly to its feet and trotted deliberately off, leaving Verrill staring after it, too surprised to make a move.

Man, however, to the majority of jaguars, must be an unknown quantity, to be treated with curiosity, caution or indifference, but only exceptionally as prey; and the scent of man holds no significance for the ordinary jaguar. G. M. Dyott was sleeping alone on a *playa* on the Maranon when a jaguar walked over his prostrate form, sniffed around, and sat down near by. Fountain did not fear to sleep on the ground, rolled in a blanket, when on the Purus, though taking the precaution of retreating a mile or more from the river for fear of caimans: 'As to jaguars and pumas, I am too well acquainted with the habits of these animals to think there is the slightest chance of their attacking sleeping men.'

Paul Le Cointe knew of no instance of a man being attacked by a jaguar, unless it or its cubs had previously been wounded; and he told Hakon Mielche in 1946 of one of his experiences, when he and a companion had pitched camp a little way in from the river. Hanging their mosquito-net over a thick branch that projected over the camp they lay down, but just as they were falling asleep they heard, in the stillness, twigs cracking under the paws of some large animal, and then the scraping of claws against bark just above their heads. Twigs and leaves spattered down on the mosquito-net. Not daring to speak, they just lay and listened for the sound of breathing that came regularly from the darkness above until, exhausted, they fell into a deep sleep. When they woke it was broad daylight, and from the marks in the bark and the tracks on the sand they saw that they had shared their camp with a large jaguar. It had come down its usual path to the river to drink, but finding its way blocked by the camp, had stopped and sniffed around to discover what this was. Then it had settled down on the branch to wait patiently until the path was clear, but had finally leaped down and gone off peacefully to look for an undisturbed drinking place.

By day the average jaguar is as pacifically disposed towards man as by night. One evening, when Alfred Wallace was on the Rio Negro, a large jet-black jaguar came out of the forest some 20yd ahead of him: 'In the middle of the road he turned his head, and for an instant he paused and gazed at me, but walked steadily on, and disappeared in the thicket. As he advanced, I heard the scampering of small animals, and the whizzing flight of ground birds.'

More than a century later Yves Manciet was waiting in the undergrowth for the sun to set when a branch cracked behind him:

> I turned round to find a jaguar coming out of the thicket; I was downwind of him and he had not smelt me; but he saw me. He was perhaps six yards away, an easy leap for such an animal. He

stood motionless for about ten seconds, tense and ready to spring, staring at me with his golden eyes. I saw the muscles rippling beneath his coat, and knew perfectly well that one bound would bring him upon me before I could even move. I went cold with fear.

All at once his muscles relaxed; he stood there looking at me nonchalantly for a moment and then turned his back and sauntered calmly off.

More often, perhaps, in such diurnal encounters, the man will be warned not to take liberties—as in the case of the jaguar, crouching with body swaying from side to side (brilliantly spotted hide shining between the palms of an interlaced thicket), which Schomburgk encountered near Tiekusi. Hissing repeatedly, eyes glaring metallic-green, the jaguar warned him off the agouti he was eating. On another occasion, when in the Priara region, Schomburgk was watching sting-rays on the sandy bottom of a stream when he heard a deep snarling and growling, and looked up to see an immense jaguar only ten to twelve paces distant at the edge of the stream. When he retreated backwards, the jaguar continued to stare at him, eyes sparkling and rolling, teeth bared, hissing and snarling. Consider also Belt's experience when near Santo Domingo: 'Seeing a large animal moving among the thick bushes, only a few yards from me, I stopped, when, to my amazement, out stalked a jaguar. He was lashing his tail, at every roar showing his great teeth. To steady my aim, if he approached me, I knelt down on one knee, supporting my left elbow on the other. He was just opposite me at the time, the movement caught his eye, he turned half round as if he were going to spring; but the next moment he turned away from me, and was lost to sight among the bushes.'

Wallace was told by Indians that some jaguars, on encountering a man, would continue quietly on their way (providing that he was not accompanied by dogs), occasionally turning to look at him and breaking into a trot if he pressed too closely. Others would face a man boldly, springing forward until within a few feet of him, and attacking if he were unwise to turn his back. No doubt a jaguar sometimes mistakes a man for legitimate prey, and there have been instances of Indians, when 'calling' deer or agoutis, being pounced on and killed by jaguars. Beebe describes how he and his companions were charged by a jaguar when only a short distance from their research station at Bartica in British Guiana. However, when only 8ft from them, the jaguar swerved and swept aside. Shortly after this experience two of them were resting in a patch of reeds while the third was working some distance ahead, when there came a sudden growl and rush: 'Instinctively we rose on the instant, just in time to see a jaguar swerve off to one side and disappear in a swish of sway-ing reed stems.' Beebe's comment on these incidents was that he had never known a jaguar to attack a man, and that in these instances the jaguar had undoubtedly heard but not scented them, and had terminated its attack immediately it had realised its mistake.

Nicholas Guppy's companion in British Guiana, a Scots-Macusi half-breed, knew of only one instance of a man being killed by a jaguar: 'Usually if it hears you coming it will go away.' Oddly enough, however, the half-breed asserted that deer-tigers (pumas) were liable to jump on a man from behind; and he apparently differentiated between the behaviour of the ordinary spotted jaguar and the black variety, as indicated by Guppy's account of his experience when he was sitting on a rock beside the Shurucanyi waterfalls in Taruma:

> Near me there was a rustling and scuffling, as of animals playing, but I could see nothing. Then with loud scratchings a black jaguar slithered down the trunk of a tree some thirty yards away, and leaped off on to the ground. It ran in a half-circle around me, then stopped. Projecting from behind the bushes I could see its hind-quarters and long thin lashing tail, then, as it crawled low, its head: it was watching me intently, with yellow eyes and flattened ears. A moment, and it ran on again for a few yards, and again stopped half-hidden, but now much nearer. I turned, keeping my face to it and wondering what to do. I could see it more clearly: it stood about three feet high, and its back was about four and a half feet long—a very big jaguar indeed.
> There was more rustling on my left, where it had come from,

and I realised that another might be approaching. At that moment it rushed off with a violence that was quite startling, and I heard the voices of men.

'Sir!" said Jonah, horrified, 'that was a lucky escape. If we had not come you would be dead now. That is a Maipuri tiger, which is the worst kind.'*

It is difficult to determine whether there is any real evidence that black jaguars are bolder by nature or, for that matter, normally larger, than spotted ones. Verrill found black jaguars greatly feared by the Indians in Costa Rica, and while he was at Atenas one killed two cows and carried off a half-grown heifer in the course of one night. A black jaguar sprang at Norwood and his companion from a distance of 30ft when they were exploring some ruins in the jungle. But this was a crippled beast, with one foreleg badly deformed from the effects of an old wound, and with festering sores on its gums, possibly as a result of an encounter with a porcupine, that *bête-noir* of the Indian tiger.

Even when attacked or wounded a jaguar may not necessarily charge. Look at his feet—was Sacha Siemel's maxim: 'A tiger must have his paws free if he is going to spring.' When Waterton's party approached a large jaguar which was standing, roaring, on the trunk of an old mora tree leaning out over a river in Demerara, it growled and bared its teeth; but on being fired at, instantly made off, though unwounded. Similarly, when Spruce's two trackers were hunting agouti one evening through a forest on the Rio Negro, they came up with a jaguar which was apparently also on the agouti's trail. Although on one of the hunter's misfiring, the jaguar advanced towards him, it retreated on being severely wounded by his companion. However, Sacha Siemel had no doubts about the ferocity of a wounded jaguar, and told Duguid that in no circumstances would he spend a night in the forest with a wounded jaguar, unless he had a torch. General Rondon stated that jaguars often charged savagely when at bay, and one of his hunters was killed when following a jaguar through thick grass. Fountain's axiom

* Since Maipouri is the Creole word for a tapir, its use in this context is obscure.

was that: 'Travellers should be very cautious in landing on thickly wooded islands in mid-stream, for the jaguar is a dangerous animal and has the habit of voluntarily attacking human beings, deliberately springing down like a flash of light from the branches of an overhanging tree where, lying stretched out on a limb, he is so perfectly camouflaged as to be invisible to the eye of a white man.'

There is no confirmation of jaguars deliberately preying on men in this way, though both J. W. B. Whetham in Central America and Leonard Clark in Yucatan referred to men being attacked by man-eaters springing on them from behind and crushing their skulls or biting through their spines. Although it is generally affirmed that there is no authentic case of a healthy, unwounded jaguar making an unprovoked attack on a man, Indians from widely dispersed regions of South America might not agree with this claim; and there can be no doubting the general dread in which jaguars are held by *caboclos* and *seringueios*. We have already noted the case of the advance-guard of a road-construction gang who, when working outside Manaos, refused to continue working because of the presence of 'a pair of tigers', despite the fact that there was no evidence that they were man-eaters.

From the old explorers, such as Stevenson, we learn that jaguars were in the habit of lingering about villages at night, waiting for men to leave their houses. We find this statement repeated about jaguars in the Nahuel Huapi national park in the west of Argentina: 'It is very bold in its desire to feed on human flesh, as it has done innumerable times, circling villages during entire nights in hope of waylaying human beings.' This recalls the assertion of the Boteudos on the Averanha that jaguars were generally man-eaters, and would follow a man for a whole day, awaiting an opportunity to kill. Stevenson added that in Gauyaquil jaguars were known to attack men when hungry and might then become man-eaters: but in that case were soon killed by common effort—a pointer to one reason why the incidence of man-eating by jaguars in populated areas has never reached proportions in any way comparable to that among tigers.

Schomburgk stated that there were authentic cases of Indian children being seized by jaguars, and that the settlements of the Arekuna in Guyana were protected by palisades. In this respect von Humboldt cites a remarkable incident related to him by a missionary, concerning two children who were playing at the edge of a forest overlooking a small corner of the great savanna region of southern Venezuela:

Suddenly a jaguar burst from the woods and began leaping back and forth, making huge bounds as it circled about them. Tiring of these manoeuvres, it hid in the grass, playfully arching its back and lowering its head, and then sprang toward them in precisely the same way as a domestic cat would have done. At last it became bolder and began leaping against the children, still in a playful manner, however. In so doing, it clawed one of the youngsters on the forehead and on the top of the head. At this the other child picked up a stick, hit the jaguar over the head, and it ran away.

Von Humboldt visited the children soon after the incident, examined the wounds, and verified the details.

Schomburgk also stated that the Indians on the Tuarutu and Vindana ranges told him that jaguars would attack men as readily as they would cattle or tapirs. About the same time von Tschudi reported that the number of jaguars had increased so greatly and had done so much damage in parts of Peru that the Indians were being compelled to move their settlements, and he cited the particular case of the village of Mayumarea, near the road to Anco, which had been abandoned for more than one hundred years because of the depredations of man-eating jaguars. This recalls a mid-nineteenth century account of life in a district of rural India terrorized by a man-eating tiger: 'The villagers lived in barricaded houses, and only stirred abroad when necessarily compelled in large bodies, covered by armed men, and beating drums and shouting as they passed along the roads. Many villages had been utterly deserted, and the whole country was evidently being slowly depopulated by this single animal.'

A decade after von Tschudi, Wallace recorded a case of a jaguar entering an Indian's house and attacking a man in a hammock; and W. L. Herndon another of a Quichua Indian on the

I

Espiritu Santo river (near Rio de Janeiro) being obliged to sleep
in a loft because of repeated nocturnal visits by jaguars. Im Thurn
also noted that the Indians in Guiana were very afraid of jaguars
which, they said, carried off dogs, children and old women from
their houses. But though the Indians in his party would sling
their hammocks in trees, after making fires round their roots,
and though he himself experienced jaguars prowling around his
own hammock slung at ground level, he knew of no instance
of one attacking in such circumstances.

None of these Indian reports of killer and man-eating jaguars
indicates whether they were driven to this abnormal behaviour
by hunger or wounds, or by some physical abnormality that
prevented them from stalking and killing their natural prey,
though the implications are that in most instances these were
healthy, though no doubt hungry, jaguars. To these can be
added Lieut Maw's hearsay account of a jaguar, probably of the
black variety, which was in the habit of walking at midday into
the plaza of a Peruvian *pueblo* and seizing the first person it
could secure, carrying off some fifty people in this manner before
it was finally shot. And Azara's statement that: 'It is certain, that
since I have been in Paraguay, the few remaining [jaguars] in
this country have devoured six men, carrying off two of them
from the midst of companions who were warming themselves
by the fire.' And Darwin's, that many woodcutters were killed
on the Parana, and that jaguars would even enter ships at night.
In confirmation of this he cited the case of a man 'now living in
the Bajada, who, coming up from below when it was dark, was
seized on the deck; he escaped, however, with the loss of an arm.'

When Darwin adds that jaguars were most dangerous when
driven from islands by floods, he was perhaps referring to an
incident that had occurred in 1825 at the Convent of San
Francisco on the Rio Grande (or Rio Bravo as it was then
known) eighteen miles from Santa Fe. On 10 April that year a
lay brother, after having made confession and concluded his
prayers, entered the sacristy. There he was terror-stricken on
opening the door to find himself face to face with a jaguar of
very extraordinary size:

In a moment the poor man was in the clutches of the beast, which dragged its victim into a back corner to finish the bloody work.

The guardian of the convent, on hearing the exclamations in the sacristy, hurried to enter the fatal room, and had scarcely become aware of what had happened when the animal leaped upon his second victim and despatched him with the same promptitude as the first.

After a while several other men attempted to enter the bloody sacristy, but not without meeting a similar fate, for the first one opening the door was immediately slain.

A senator, Mr Iriondo, being present, tried now to approach the sacristy by an adjoining back room which communicated with the former by a small door. The jaguar, however, had left the sacristy in the meantime through the very door which Mr Iriondo wanted to use, and before the latter, followed by a small crowd, could enter it, he heard cries, 'Here he is! Here he goes! Save me!' With this the roaring of the jaguar was heard, and mingled with it the last exclamations of a fourth victim.

There were, of course, special reasons for this macabre incident, inasmuch as the convent was laid out on the banks of the river, which occasionally overflowed islets in front of the town. On this occasion all animals, including the jaguar, had been driven off the islands and the jaguar had entered the convent garden, which was encircled towards the river by a low wall. It entered the sacristy through a small door which had accidentally been left open at the back of the convent; and when the men entered from the front of the convent, the jaguar found its retreat cut off by the flooded river.

These accounts bear the stamp of truth, as does another by Richard Spruce of an incident that occurred a few years before he arrived at Santana in 1850, the victim of which was wearing a skull-cap because he still felt the effects of his wound. In this instance a jaguar had sprung from the bush on to one of two men. The victim, being a powerful man, seized the jaguar by its forepaws initially; but it eventually freed one paw and scalped him. Then it sat down between the two men, looking from one to the other. On the third member of the party arriving on the scene, he was able to kill the jaguar, despite also being wounded.

There is little recent evidence of man-eating, and Leopold states that there are no authentic cases in Mexico—though this must exclude Yucatan. But Siemel, though finding most jaguars shy of men, states that one encounters an occasional man-killer: usually a female who, after killing an Indian in defence of her cubs, and sampling his flesh, realises that men are easy prey and becomes a confirmed man-eater. Drawing a parallel with man-eating tigers, it is possible that the cubs of such a jaguar may themselves become man-eaters by emulation, though there is no evidence of this. Prado describes how, when he was a young man, he was asked to kill a man-eater in the lower Aripiana region, which he suspected to be a female with an injured paw and the mate of a male that had been killed a few months earlier. In twenty days this beast had killed six people, the last of whom had been a woman washing clothes near her house. Her screams and the snarling of her dogs, two of whom were mangled to death, attracted the attention of two woodmen, but the jaguar, leaving the hapless woman, turned and drove them off. When they returned with reinforcements it had disappeared with the woman's body.

This female was known to be feeding cubs, as she had previously been seen to drag part of a stag into a den near the foot of a waterfall. This was a new lair to which she had moved after taking to man-eating; and Prado found the waterfall to be beside a pool, where stags and 'elks' had recently been drinking. Though flanked by rocks and jujube trees, it was in comparatively open country of ferns, cacti and thorn bushes, which were noisy with toucans, macaws and parrots. After lying out all night he glimpsed the female with her two cubs for a fraction of a second in a thicket at dawn. Later in the morning the heat of the sun, together with the knowledge that the jaguar was probably away hunting in the forest, lulled Prado into a doze. Subsequently he roused himself for a smoke, and was sitting in the shade, with his rifle by his side, when some pebbles fell on his feet. After glancing at them in an incurious way he looked up to see where they came from: 'Instantly, I forgot the cigarette, snatched at the rifle and endeavoured to get to my feet, thinking even as I did so, "Too late," for there, only a few feet above me, was the jaguar and the two cubs playing at her side. The cubs continued to frolic, knocking down pebbles, but the mother had already seen me, and was gathering herself to jump. In less time than it takes to tell she was hurtling through the air. She was an enormous mass and I could see the white marking which covered her chest as she went into the parabola of the bound.' After he had shot her, Prado found that there was a deep scar on the pad of her right front paw.

Roosevelt was told by an Argentine captain on the Boundary Commission of a jaguar that entered his camp several times in quest of their dried beef. When this was finally removed out of its reach the jaguar, moving so quietly that it did not alarm the dogs, seized one of his men at midnight and killed him by driving its fangs through his skull. It dropped the man during the subsequent uproar and escaped, but when bayed by the dogs the next morning and killed, proved to be a large male in excellent condition. So, also, was another large male long known to be dangerous when attacked, which was trapped in the Chaco after killing three people and eating two of them.

Of other recent instances of man-killing, Senor Abren (a Campeche mahogany and shipping tycoon) gave Leonard Clark an account of a man in an ox-cart who was attacked at high noon by a small female jaguar, weighing less than 150lb, and dragged into the bush. The two were found some hours later: the jaguar dead by strangulation, and the man unconscious and subsequently dying. Clark himself mentions a three-legged man-eater in the Opaxta district of Yucatan, which had killed five mission men over a period of months, making the rounds of the district every seven or eight days, in typical tiger fashion; and while in the cemetery at La Merced he counted thirty-two crosses over the graves of men killed by man-eaters hunting singly or in pairs. In his opinion these man-eaters were either wounded animals or mentally unbalanced by the torture of ant-bites; but one suspects that many of these graves may, in fact, have been those of victims, not of jaguars, but of their fellow men: just as in India the presence of a man-eating tiger often provided villagers with the cover for settling scores with an enemy.

11

Jaguars—Past and Present

Today, the jaguars' range has contracted somewhat; but because man has not yet penetrated vast areas of the South American hinterland, they have not suffered the fate of the cats of the Old World. It can be safely assumed that, in the northern parts of their range, they have never at any time been numerous north of Mexico. No jaguar has been known to breed in California since John Capen Adams' record in 1855, and there are no records of their breeding in New Mexico or Arizona, though in 1932 E. A. Goldman described them as regular residents (*sic*) in south-eastern Arizona. Nor do there appear to be any breeding records for Texas, though since they were apparently common in the 1840s along the Guadeloupe and the Rio Grande, it would be most surprising if some had not bred in the more congenial environment of tropical south-east Texas with its great herds of wild cattle and mustangs.

It was in the summer of 1855 that Adams, accompanied by his dog and two tame grizzlies, 'Lady Washington' and 'Ben Franklin', was hunting in the Tehachapi mountains on a slope facing east over the Mojave desert. At midnight he was suddenly aroused by a fearful snuffling and snorting from his grizzlies. Although it was starlight it was too dark to see, but he distinctly heard the lapping of water at a spring about 50yd from his camp and, looking in that direction, saw two spots, like balls of fire, glaring at him, which he recognised as the eyes that had previously frightened his horse. He prepared to meet an attack; but the stranger—which he could now make out to be 'a large animal of the lion genus'—unexpectedly, after uttering a low growl, turned and retreated leisurely.

As soon as it was light the next morning Adams set out to follow its trail, which led him four or five miles over rough country spattered with huge rocks, but with here and there patches of soft earth carrying pug-marks, and finally into a gorge —one of the roughest and craggiest places he had ever set eyes on. The track crossed the gorge and led up to a cave on a rock ledge on the side of the cliff. In the mouth of the cave, and scattered below it, were multitudes of bones and skeletons of various kinds of animals, including mountain sheep.

A few nights later, Adams had barely closed his eyes when he was roused by a roar, which was repeated less loudly a few minutes later; and in the pale light of a new moon he saw a spotted animal resembling a puma (with which he was of course, very familiar) in form and size, with two young ones, crawling out of the rocks. Having advanced a little way from the cave, 'she turned round and appeared to call the little ones, which followed, playing like kittens'.

On another night:

> The male animal again made its appearance. As he came to the mouth of the den, he looked around and snuffed the air, and then leaped down, and going a few yards placed his paws upon a rock, and stretched himself, yawning at the same time, as if he were waking out of a sleep. A few minutes afterward the female appeared, and approaching, lapped his brawny neck. Pleased with this conjugal attention, the male threw himself upon the ground, and after rolling for a few minutes, stood up, shook himself, and then, with a proud step, trod away; and his consort followed him.

Some five years after this experience of Adams, an Indian (camouflaged with a deer's antlers) was attacked by, and killed, a jaguar when stalking deer near Palm Spring. In the 1920s W. S. Strong was told by the old chief of the Cahuilla Indians, who inhabited the Coachello Valley and the San Jacinto and Santa Rosa mountains, that in the days of his youth he had been well acquainted with a large cat with a spotted yellow-brown skin and a long tail that lived in the mountains bordering the

desert at Cahuilla. His people were in the habit of following the
tracks of this cat (known to them as Tu'kwut), and also of pumas
(Tu'kwit), in order to uncover the carcasses of deer buried by
them; but the names jaguar and El Tigre were unknown to him.

These old records may be compared with that given to H. C.
Merriam by the chief of the Kamei—that the 'tiger' was known
(though rare) to his ancestors in the mountain region of Guy-
maca as Hut-te-kul, the big-spotted lion. J. G. Pattie also refers
to an animal like a leopard that was to be found on islands in
the delta of the Colorado in 1883. But there do not appear to
have been any subsequent records of a jaguar ranging as far
north-west as California until that of the already mentioned
Baja male in 1955. It is as an infrequent wanderer that the jaguar
is known today in the western USA—to the Rincon and Babo-
quivari Mountains of Arizona just north of the Mexican border,
and on the scrub-covered hills south-west of Tucson, where one
is occasionally killed by Indians some fifty miles north of the
border.

Although jaguars are reported to have been greatly reduced in
numbers, or exterminated, in the more highly developed parts
of Mexico's tropical lowlands, they are still numerous in the
wilder country. J. F. Ferreira, who had killed sixty jaguars up to
1959, had not noted any diminution in their numbers during his
lifetime in such traditional localities as the coastal mangrove
swamps between Nayarit and Guerrero and the forested, well-
watered lowlands and foothills of the Sierra Madre in southern
Sinoloa; and it was in these areas and in the still extensive Gulf
coast rain-forests, as far west as the central Campeche and as
far north as the Rio Grande, that Leopold found the highest
densities of jaguars during his 1958 survey. There is a persistent
rumour that there exists in the western lowlands, from south of
Sonora to Nayarit, a third large cat, neither jaguar nor puma nor
jaguarundi, known as the *onza* or *ounce*. It is reported to be about
the size of a puma with faint shoulder stripes, and to leave
elongated pug-marks in contrast to the round pugs of other cats.

Belt saw only one jaguar in Nicaragua, and Whetham recorded only two in Guatemala: but other travellers have found

them common enough in all the Central American states (and also in Yucatan) except Salvador, where they perhaps became extinct in the 1920s. But did the cutting of the Panama Canal affect their distribution? And has there always been a traffic of jaguars between South America and Mexico?

Some authorities have concluded that there has been little contraction of the jaguar's range in South America since the time of the Conquistadores: others that jaguars have been decimated or exterminated by hunting in the north and south of their range. It has been widely stated that they were to be found as far south as the Magellan Strait until the late eighteenth century, and the remains of a very large one are reported to have been found in the Cueva Ebergardt; while early accounts refer to Patagonia being infested with 'water tigers'. It is also true that there are a remarkable number of place-names in the far south of South America in which the word 'Nahuel', or jaguar, is employed in association with rivers, lakes, islands and even farms. No fewer than forty-three have been located in the province of Buenos Aires, twenty-nine of which refer to watercourses or other aquatic sites; the most widely known national park in Argentina is Nahuel Huapi or Tiger Island; there is a Nahuel Buta deep in Chile; and the great lake of Isle Victoria in the south of Patagonia was formerly also known as Nahuel Huapi. Patagonia is the country of the Auracan Indians, and Nahuel plays a great part in their legends, as we have seen the jaguar to do in that of most Indian peoples; but Dr Dennler de La Tour informs me that 'Nahuel' is not, in fact, an Auracanian word, but originated as a family name among the Tuelehe Indians of the pampas, and that there is no evidence that jaguars ranged as far south as the Auracans' country.

He goes on to point out that the use of the word 'tiger' or *tigre* for jaguar in South American literature has been a source of perpetual confusion, since in Spanish as in French *tigre* is the equivalent of fierce or strong, and may be employed as appropriately to an outstanding tango-dancer as to a jaguar or any other strong and 'savage' animal. In his history of the Abipones, a tribe inhabiting the most northerly part of Argentina, Martin

Dobizhoffer, a German Jesuit, referred for example to the 'water tiger' in these words: 'In the deepest waters there usually hides an animal larger than any hunting-dog, called *tigre de agua* by the Spaniards and *yaquaro* by the Guaranos. It has a woolly hide, a long and tapering tail, and powerful claws. Horses and mules swimming across these rivers are dragged to the bottom. Soon afterwards one sees the intestines of the animal, disembowelled by the tiger, floating to the surface.' But this is, in fact, an exact description of the giant otter, coupled with the predatory activities of the *yacare* or caiman.

It will be recalled that Azara stated that two thousand jaguars were killed annually in the valley of the La Plata during the early years of the Spaniards. By the late eighteenth century they had, according to him, been so persecuted that they were to be found only in riverine jungles and woods and in the desert area of Paraguay. Some years before Darwin's visit in 1832, they had been exterminated in the Maldonaldo in the north Plata, although they were still to be found in the reed-jungles bordering the lakes to the south—where Hudson found them abundant on the Saladillo a few years later—and also on the wooded banks of the great rivers in the Parana to the north. By von Humboldt's day in the mid-nineteenth century four thousand skins were being exported annually from the Spanish colonies, and by the early years of the twentieth century the jaguars in Uruguay had been exterminated by cattle ranchers.

One would have wished to conclude this sadly incomplete account of the natural history of jaguars with some assessment of their present status and future prospects but, as in the case of the majority of South American animals, the necessary data do not exist. No doubt it will be a very, very long time before the vast jungle areas of South America are opened up, though airstrips and transcontinental highways are biting into them. Nevertheless, even from such relatively inaccessible regions as the upper Amazon comes deeply disquieting evidence of excessive hunting pressures in those areas lying within thirty miles or so of the major river highways. In 1966, according to Ian Grimwood, the Technical Wildlife Adviser to the Peruvian

Government, skins traded at Iquitos included the shocking totals of 15,000 ocelots, 4,000 margays and tiger-cats, 55,000 deer and 220,000 peccaries, in addition to 891 jaguars and 210 giant otters, despite the fact that the latter have been almost exterminated in Peru, and also in Brazil, since at $1,800 a skin they command the highest prices in the South American fur market.

In that year also the Director-General of the Valle State Museum in Colombia stated that he had in his possession the records of one trader who was exporting 480,000 skins a year; while during the first eight months of 1968, 7,238 jaguar skins, valued at $864,000, were imported by the USA (including 4,473 from Brazil, 677 from Colombia and 397 from Mexico). But while tens of thousands of South American animals are being slaughtered annually for their skins, as many more are being butchered for the meat trade. The fishy-flavoured carcass of the capybara, for example, is actually sold as fish, sometimes under the name of salmon; and the above-mentioned Director-General cites an instance of Venezuelan traders seeking permission to slaughter 300,000 capybara a year in Colombia: 'On my advice, the Minister of Agriculture refused. The Venezuelans then brought a little pressure on another minister, and he got them a permit quota for 20,000. But there is no control. The animals are herded into corrals and clubbed to death for their meat; the valuable skin is removed and thrown away.'

No less a threat to the smaller fauna of Amazonia is presented by the pet trade, especially that passing through Miami, Florida. Live monkeys are exported from Iquitos, at the rate of 50,000 each year, and the trade in monkeys from Peru alone is large enough to support a special weekly flight from Iquitos to Miami, while that from Colombia and Venezuela, and perhaps also from Brazil and Ecuador, may be even greater.

Scientific Names of Animals mentioned in Text

Black Spider Monkey	*Ateles ater*
Red Howler Monkey	*Alouatta seniculus*
Spectacled Bear	*Tremarctos ornatus*
Jaguar	*Panthera onca*
Tiger	*Panthera tigris*
Leopard	*Panthera pardus*
Puma	*Puma concolor*
Ocelot	*Leopardus pardalis*
Giant Otter	*Pteronura brasiliensis*
Coati	*Nasua (spp)*
Giant Anteater	*Myrmecophaga tridactyla*
Lesser Anteater	*Tamandua tetradactyla*
Three-toed Sloth	*Bradypus tridactylus*
Two-toed Sloth	*Choloepus (spp)*
Porcupine	*Coendou prehensilis (Echinoprocta rufescens)*
Agouti	*Dasyprocta (spp)*
Paca (Labba)	*Cuniculus paca*
Capybara	*Hydrochoerus hydrochaeris*
Tapir	*Tapirus (spp)*
Peccary, Collared	*Tayassu angulatus*
Peccary, White-lipped	*Tayassu pecari*
Deer, Marsh	*Blastocerus dichotomus*
Deer, Pampas	*Blastocerus bezoarticus*
Deer, White-tailed	*Odocoileus virginianus*

Brocket	*Mazama (spp)*
Manatee	*Trichelus inunguis*
Anaconda	*Eunectes (spp)*
Boa Constrictor	*Constrictor (spp)*
Bushmaster	*Lachesis muta*
Caiman	*Caiman (spp)*
Crocodile	*Crocodylus (spp)*
Turtle, River	*Podocnemis expansa*
Arapaima (Pirarucu)	*Arapaima gigas*
Piranha (Perai, Caribe)	*Serrasalmus (spp)*

Bibliography

NOTE: The literature of exploration in South America includes a vast deal of tedious travelogue and very little about jaguars—as I have painfully discovered. I have, therefore, restricted this bibliography mainly to works that can be read with profit by naturalists interested in the larger fauna.

Azara, F. de, *The Natural History of the Quadrupeds of Paraguay*, Edinburgh, 1838

Bates, H. W., *The Naturalist on the River Amazon*, 1863

Bates, M., *The Land and Wildlife of South America*, 1964

Beebe, C. W., *Our Search for a Wilderness*, New York, 1910
 Tropical Wild Life in British Guiana, New York, 1917
 Jungle Peace, New York, 1919
 Jungle Days, New York, 1925
 Edge of the Jungle, New York, 1921

Belt, T., *The Naturalist in Nicaragua*, 1874

Bertam, G. C. L., *In Search of Mermaids*, 1963

Bigg-Wither, T. P., *Pioneering in South Brazil*, 1878

Blomberg, R., *Buried Gold and Anacondas*, 1959
 Chavante, 1960

Boddam-Whetham, J. W., *Across Central America*, 1877

Brown, C. B., *Canoe and Camp Life in British Guiana*, 1876

Burton, M., *Systematic Dictionary of Mammals of the World*, 1965

Cabrera, A. & Yepes, J., *Historia Natural edjar Mammiferos sud-Americanos*, Buenos Aires, 1940

Cahalane, V., *Mammals of North America*, New York, 1947

Carpenter, C. R., *Field Study of Behaviour and Social Relations of*

   Howling Monkeys, Comparative Psychology Monographs, John Hopkins Press, vol 10, no 2, 1934
Carr, A., *The Turtle*, 1968
Chapman, F. M., *Life in an Air Castle*, 1938
   My Tropical Air Castle, 1929
Cherrie, G. K., *Dark Trails*, New York, 1930
Clark, L., *The Rivers ran East*, 1954
   Yucatan Adventure, 1959
Cordan, W., *Secret of the Forest*, 1963
Cutright, P. R., *Great Naturalists explore South America*, New York, 1940
Darwin, C., *A Naturalist's Voyage round the World in HMS Beagle*, 1890
De Leeuw, H., *Crossroads of the Caribbean Sea*, New York, 1935
Dickey, H. S., *My Jungle Book*, Boston, 1932
Dinsdale, T., *The Leviathans*, 1966
Duguid, J., *Green Hell*, 1931
   Tiger-Man, 1932
Dyott, G. M., *Man-Hunting in the Jungle*, Indianapolis, 1930
Earl, S., *The Hills of the Boasting Woman*, 1962
Egli, E., in *The Amazon* (Schulthess, E.), 1962
Fabre, D. G., *Beyond the River of the Dead*, 1926
Falkner, T., *A Description of Patagonia*, 1774
Fawcett, P. H., *Exploration Fawcett*, 1953
Fiedler, A., *River of Singing Fish*, 1951
Fife, C. W. D., *Among the Wild Tribes of the Amazon*, 1924
Fitter, R., *Vanishing Wild Animals of the World*, 1968
Fleming, P., *Brazilian Adventure*, 1933
Flornoy, B., *Inca Adventure*, 1956
Fountain, P., *Mountains and Forests of South America*, 1902
   The River Amazon, 1914
Friel, A. O., *The River of Seven Stars*, New York, 1924
Gadow, H. F., *Through Southern Mexico*, 1908
Gardner, G., *Travels in Brazil*, 1849
Goldman, E. A., 'Jaguars of North America', *Proc. Biol. Soc. Washington*, vol. 45, 1932

Gudger, E. W., 'Jaguar Fishing with Tail,' *Journal of Mammalogy*, vol 27, no 1, 1946
  'Cats as Fishermen,' Natural History, 1925
Guenther, K., *A Naturalist in Brazil*, Boston, 1931
Guppy, N., *Wai- Wai*, 1958
Hanson, E. P., *Journey to Manaos*, New York, 1938
Herndon, W. L. & Gibbon, L., *Explorations of the Valley of the Amazon*, 1854
Heuvelmans, B., *On the Track of Unknown Animals*, 1958
Hudson, W. H., *The Naturalist in La Plata*, 1892
Humboldt, Baron A. von, *Travels to the Equinoctial Regions of the New Continent*, 1852
Im Thurn, E. F., *Among the Indians of Guiana*, 1883
Jolly, S., *South American Adventures*, 1928
Kerr, Sir J. G., *A Naturalist in the Gran Chaco*, 1950
Lange, A., *The Lower Amazon*, New York, 1914
  In the Amazon Jungle, New York, 1912
La Cordière, Th., 'Moeurs des Jaguars de l'Amerique due Sud,' *Revue des Deux Mondes*, vol 8, Paris, 1832
Le Cointe, P., *L'Amazonie Bresilienne*, Paris, 1922
Leopold, A. S., *Wildlife of Mexico*, University of California Press, 1960
MacCreagh, G., *White Waters and Black*, 1927
McBride, B. St. J., *Amazon Journey*, 1959
Manciet, Y., *Land of Tomorrow: An Amazon Journey*, 1964
Masterman, G. F., *Seven Eventful Years in Paraguay*, 1869
Matthiessen, P., *The Cloud Forest*, 1962
Maufrais, R., *Matto Grosso Adventure*, 1955
Maw, Lieut H. L., *Journal of a Passage from the Pacific to the Atlantic*, 1829
McGovern, W. M., *Jungle Paths and Inca Ruins*, 1925
Merriam, C. H., 'Jaguar in California', *Journal of Mammalogy*, vol 1, no 1, 1919
Metraux, A., 'The Native Tribes of Eastern Bolivia and Western Mato Grosso,' *Bull. Bur. Amer. Ethn. Soc.* 134, 1943
Meyer, G., *Summer at High Altitude*, 1968
  The River and the People, 1966

Mielche, H., *The Amazon*, 1949

Miller, F. W., 'Mammals from Southern Matto Grosso,' *Journal of Mammalogy*, vol 2, 1930

Miller, L. E., *In the Wilds of South America*, 1919

Moore, J. H., *Tears of the Sun God*, 1965

Morton, F., *Xelahuk*, 1959

Nelson, E. W., 'Wild Animals of North America,' Washington, 1930

Nelson, E. W., & Goldman, E. A., in *Journal of Mammalogy*, vol 14, no 3, 1933

Noice, H. H., *Back of Beyond*, 1939

Norwood, V. G. C., *Drums along the Amazon*, 1964

Osgood, W. H., 'Mammals of an Expedition across North Peru,' *Field Museum Nat. Hist. Zoo. Ser. Publ. 176*, 10 (12), 1914

Paez, R., *Travels and Adventures in South and Central America*, New York, 1868

Peissel, M., *The Lost World of Quintana Roo*, New York, 1963

Perry, R., *The World of the Tiger*, 1964

Pinney, R., *Vanishing Tribes*, 1968

Pope, C. H., *Giant Snakes*, 1962

Prado, E. B., *The Lure of the Amazon*, 1959

Prodgers, C. H., *Adventures in Bolivia*, 1922

Rengger, J. R., *Naturgeschichte der Säugetiere von Paraguay*, Basle, 1830

Reuss, P. A., *The Amazon Trail*, 1954

Rice, A. H., *El Rio Negro*, 1934

Roosevelt, E., *Through the Brazilian Wilderness*, 1914

Rusby, H. H., *Jungle Memories*, New York, 1933

Salaman, R. N., *The History and Social Influence of the Potato*, 1949

Sandeman, C., *A Forgotten River*, 1939

Schomburgk, R., *Travels in British Guiana*, 1922

Schurz, W. L., *Brazil: The Infinite Country*, 1962

Seitz, G., *People of the Rain-forests*, 1963

Seton, E. T., *Lives of Game Animals*, New York, 1929

Sowls, L. K., 'The Collared Peccary,' *Animals*, vol 12, no 5, 1969

K

Spruce, R., *Notes of a Botanist on the Amazon and Andes*, 1908

Stevenson, W. R., *Historical and Descriptive Narrative of 20 Years Residence in South America*, 1825

Strong, W. S. in *Journal of Mammalogy*, vol. 11, 1926

Swan, M., *The Marches of El Dorado*, 1958

Tate, G. H. H., in *Journal of Mammalogy*, vol. 12, no 3, 1931

Toro, A del, *Los Animales silvestres de Chiapas*, Chiapas, 1952

Tschudi, J. von, *Travels in Peru*, 1847

Turnbull-Kemp, P., *The Leopard*, 1967

Up de Graff, F. W., *Head-Hunters of the Amazon*, New York, 1927

Verrill, A. H., *Thirty Years in the Jungle*, 1929

Wallace, A. R., *Travels on the Amazon*, 1853

Waterton, C., *Wanderings in South America*, 1909

Whitney, C., *The Flowing Road*, 1912

Woodcock, G., *To the City of the Dead*, 1957

Young, S. P. & Goldman, E. A., *The Puma*, Washington, 1946

Acknowledgements

To Richard Jr who edited the MS. I am also greatly indebted to the County Libraries of Devon and Cornwall for providing me with an immense number of books, and to their reference departments for bibliographical assistance; also to Dr Dennler de La Tour of Buenos Aires; and to the following authors and publishers for permission to quote from their books: Jonathan Cape, *Green Hell* (1931) by Julian Duguid, and *White Waters and Black* (1927) by Gordon MacCreagh; Alan Ross, *The River and the People* (1966) by Gordon Meyer; Robert Hale, *Drums along the Amazon* (1964) by V. C. G. Norwood, and *Amazon Journey* (1959) by B. St J. McBride; Collins, *The Amazon* (1962) by Emil Schulthess; Allen & Unwin, *Buried Gold and Anacondas* (1959) by Rolf Blomberg; the Macmillan Company (New York), *Great Naturalists explore South America* (1940) by P. R. Cutright; Hutchinson, *Exploration Fawcett* (1953) by P. H. Fawcett; Souvenir Press, *The Lure of the Amazon* (1959) by E. B. Prado; Oliver & Boyd and Libraire Ernest Flammarion, *Land of To-morrow* (1964) by Yves Manciet; John Murray and E. P. Dutton, *Wai-Wai* (1958) by Nicholas Guppy; and Victor Gollancz, *The Secret of the Forest* (1963) by Wolfgang Cordan.

RICHARD PERRY

Northumberland, 1969

Index

description of jaguar playing with children, 141; numbers of jaguars, 150

Iguana, 103
Im Thurn, E. F., jaguar's prey, 38; jaguars as man-eaters, 142
Incas, *Royal Commentaries* and worship of jaguar, 104; territories, 107; jaguar as fertility symbol, 108; description of Pizarro reception, 118
Indian Protection Service, 113
Insects, 102, 112–13
Iquitos, 64, 151

Jaguar, derivation of name, 28, 102, 109, 149; description of, 20, 23; melanism, 20, 139; measurements, 19; voice, 17, 18, 103, 125–6; geographical range, 9, 10, 19, 20, 146, 147–50; environment, 9, 10, 12, 20, 21, 22, 24, 31, 102, 148; numbers, 150–1; territory, 12, 14; demarcation of territory, 14; nocturnalism and diurnalism, 23, 118; migrations, 12, 22; social structure, 14, 17; breeding, 15, 17, 18; interbreeding with puma, leopard, lion, 26; breeding environment, 12, 144, 147; young, 18; prey: deer, 22, 31; peccary, 26, 39, 41–3; tapir, 29, 36, 37; capybara, 47; domestic stock and dogs, 9, 129–32; sloth, 50, 53; monkey, 56; manatee, 30; small game, 25; caiman and crocodile, 62; anaconda, 74, 80, 81; turtle, 38, 65; vegetable food, 26; hunting: range, 12, 14; environment, 22; territory, 12, 14; tracks, 23; calls, 17, 18; mimicry, 28; odour, 27; equipment, 23; methods, 27, 28, 29, 36, 37, 41–3, 50, 53, 56, 62–3;

fishing, 65, 71; behaviour with kill, 29, 30; strength, 30; relations with other animals—puma, compared in numbers with, 17; hunting and territorial competition with, 26–7; fighting with, 27; wolf, 30; vulture, 30; anteater, 48; relations with man: encounters with, 24, 27, 133–7; not attacking, 23, 134–40; as man-eater, 15, 101, 140–5; hunters' methods, 117–26; captive, 127–9; as supernatural, 18, 101, 108–11, 115; as god, idol and fertility symbol, 102–8, 110–11
Jivaro Indians, jaguar as *shaman*, 18; animal gods, 35, 110; howler monkey folklore, 59

Karaja Indians, jaguar dance, 109
Kerr, J. G., frightening jaguar, 132
Koch-Grünberg, Th vom, jaguars fishing, 67

La Cordière, Th., jaguars fishing, 67
La Merced, 145
La Plata, 12, 39, 47, 66, 150
La Tour, D. de, derivations of Nahuel and *tigre*, 149
Lange, A., habits of tapir, 32; description of jaguar hunting tapir, 37; tapir under water, 38; sloth falling, 53; anacondas in numbers, 85; description of gigantic anaconda, 93
Le Cointe, P., jaguar killing caiman, 63; jaguar fishing with tail, 71; description of jaguar visiting camp, 136
Leopold, A. S., jaguar attacks on Mexican herds, 9; jaguar's hunting range, 14; nocturnal jaguars, 23; jaguar as controller of game, 25; jaguar's strength, 30; roaring of

Perry, Richard, 1909–
  The world of the jaguar. New York, Taplinger Pub. Co.
₍1970₎

  168 p. illus. (part col.), maps. 23 cm. $6.50
  Bibliography : p. 154–158.

  1. Jaguars.   ɪ. Title.

QL737.C23P38   599.7′4428   78–117933
ISBN 0-8008-8590-2   MARC

Library of Congress   70 ₍4₎